Disney

OZ
THE
GREAT
AND
POWERFUL

Disney
Oz
THE GREAT AND POWERFUL

Adapted by Elizabeth Rudnick
Based upon the screenplay by
Mitchell Kapner and David Lindsay-Abaire
Based upon the books of L. Frank Baum

Executive Producers Grant Curtis,
Palak Patel, Philip Steuer, Josh Donen
Produced by Joe Roth
Screen Story by Mitchell Kapner
Screenplay by Mitchell Kapner
and David Lindsay-Abaire
Directed by Sam Raimi

PUFFIN

For more Oz fun, visit
disney.com/thewizard

PUFFIN BOOKS

Published by the Penguin Group
Penguin Books Ltd, 80 Strand, London WC2R 0RL, England
Penguin Group (USA) Inc., 375 Hudson Street, New York, New York 10014, USA
Penguin Group (Canada), 90 Eglinton Avenue East, Suite 700, Toronto, Ontario, Canada M4P 2Y3
(a division of Pearson Penguin Canada Inc.)
Penguin Ireland, 25 St Stephen's Green, Dublin 2, Ireland (a division of Penguin Books Ltd)
Penguin Group (Australia), 707 Collins Street, Melbourne, Victoria 3008, Australia
(a division of Pearson Australia Group Pty Ltd)
Penguin Books India Pvt Ltd, 11 Community Centre, Panchsheel Park, New Delhi – 110 017, India
Penguin Group (NZ), 67 Apollo Drive, Rosedale, Auckland 0632, New Zealand
(a division of Pearson New Zealand Ltd)
Penguin Books (South Africa) (Pty) Ltd, Block D, Rosebank Office Park, 181 Jan Smuts Avenue, Parktown
North, Gauteng 2193, South Africa

Penguin Books Ltd, Registered Offices: 80 Strand, London WC2R 0RL, England

puffinbooks.com

First published by Disney Press, an imprint of Disney Book Group, 2013
Published in Great Britain by Puffin Books 2013
001

Set in Horley Old Style MT
Printed in Great Britain by Clays Ltd, St Ives plc

British Library Cataloguing in Publication Data
A CIP catalogue record for this book is available from the British Library

ISBN: 978–0–141–34903–9

www.greenpenguin.co.uk

Penguin Books is committed to a sustainable
future for our business, our readers and our planet.
This book is made from Forest Stewardship
Council™ certified paper.

ALWAYS LEARNING　　　　**PEARSON**

THE CIRCUS HAD ARRIVED IN TOWN. While it was a rather small and somewhat run-down affair, the citizens of the rural Kansas town still made their way through the gate, eager to escape their dull and gray lives if just for a few minutes and enter a world of wonder.

Horse-drawn buggies were parked outside, while farmers and their wives strolled the midway taking in the sights. A strong man accepted an iron bar from his beautiful wife and, gritting his teeth, slowly bent it. Farther down, a carnival worker shouted to passersby, encouraging them to come and see the gunslinging sharpshooting honey pie of the Wild West, Miss Bettylou Gumption. Suddenly, one voice rose above the others. It was coming from in front of a medium-sized exhibition tent.

"Right this way, folks!" the man in front of the tent called out. "Come and meet a master of magic and prestidigitation! He has traveled the world and baffled the crown princes of Europe! He will amaze! He will astound! In five short minutes the Great Oz will awaken from his deep meditative trance and the show will begin!"

Intrigued, people made their way into the tent, paying the man as they went. He smiled. It was going to be a good show.

Behind the tent, inside a wooden trailer belonging to the Great Oz, a beautiful young woman was applying her lipstick. "I always knew I was destined for show-biz. Now look at me—a magician's assistant. Just a few minutes ago I was selling oil cakes on the midway!"

"Opportunity comes when you least expect it, my dear May," said a voice that seemed to float out from behind a dressing curtain. Suddenly, the curtain parted with a dramatic flare as the voice called out, "Zim Zallah Bim!"

CHAPTER ONE

May looked up to see a man dressed in a turban and a long magician's coat standing in front of the curtain. This was Oscar Zoroaster Phadrig Isaac Norman Henkle Emmanuel Ambroise Diggs, otherwise known as the Great Oz.

"Wow, what a getup," May said. Oz smiled at his beautiful young assistant. He loved the circus life. It fit his personality to a T. He was never in one place for long, so there was always a new woman to woo or a crowd to please—and more importantly, no ties to bind him.

At that moment, Oz was in the process of training May to be a part of the act. While she wasn't the brightest star under the big top, she was infatuated with Oz and that was all that mattered—to him.

May giggled at his outfit. He cut quite the figure in his costume. His dark hair curled slightly under a tall black hat and his broad shoulders filled out the black jacket he wore. Looking over at May, his eyes twinkled mischievously, causing her to giggle even more.

Walking over, Oscar removed May's hat. "You won't need this," the magician began. "You'll be playing the 'simple country girl.'"

Then, with a flourish, he pulled his hand from

behind his back to reveal a small music box. "A gift for you," he said. "In honor of your debut. It belonged to my grandmother—a tsarina from Irkutsk and a decorated war hero."

May cocked her head. "War hero?" she repeated. "Your grand*mother*?"

Oz nodded. "She enlisted disguised as a potato farmer! Poor thing died in battle."

"How sad," May said. "Which battle?"

"Which batt—?" Oz started. May was asking too many questions. This was just another trick on Oz's part. His grandmother wasn't a war hero. It just sounded good . . . and made the ladies fall in love with him that much faster. He quickly racked his brain for an answer. "Oh, there are so many!" he finally said. "You've heard of the Battle of, uh, Kreplach?"

May shook her head.

Oz smiled. "Oh *good*! It was the Battle of Kreplach! A bloody skirmish. This box was the only thing to survive." He opened the music box and it began to play a lovely tune. "I know Grammie would want you to have it." May swooned as Oz leaned in for a kiss. . . .

"Professor!" a voice called, causing Oz to pull back and scowl. A moment later Frank, Oz's beleaguered assistant, bounded into the trailer.

4

CHAPTER ONE

"How many times have I told you to KNOCK!" Oz shouted angrily.

Frank paused, noticing May for the first time. Turning, he walked out of the trailer, shutting the door behind him.

Oz sighed. Good help was so hard to find. "You know what he's doing, don't you?" he said to May with an exhausted sigh. A moment later, there was a knock on the door. "Come in!" Oz said, rolling his eyes.

Frank re-entered. "It's showtime!" he said. "Only half a house. Here's the take." He dumped his bowler hat on a nearby table, and a few pennies, a couple of nickels, and a rabbit's foot spilled out.

Looking at all the money, or more specifically, the lack thereof, Oz's eyes flashed with annoyance. Was that all those simple farmers thought he was worth? Scooping up the meager take, he unequally divided the money, giving just a few coins to Frank and nothing to May, insisting that for her, the applause from the crowd would be payment enough. But Frank wasn't having it and began to protest.

"Well, how do you think I feel?" Oz replied. "A man of my talents! I should be playing the Orpheum Circuit! Instead, I'm in some dusty Podunk wearing a second-hand jacket that's falling apart at the seams!" Oz lifted his elbow to expose a tear in the material. "You need to patch this, by the way," he said quietly to Frank.

Oz made his way to his workbench and began the final preparations for the show. He put some flash-paper up his sleeve, a handkerchief in his pocket, and a few doves in his coat. While he was preparing for his stage act, Frank eyed May hopefully.

"So you're the new girl, huh?" he said as she smiled at him. "Good, we needed a new one. The last one left us. Poor thing suffered from a broken heart."

"Attack! Heart attack!" Oz quickly interrupted. "She's resting in Abilene and is expected to make a full recovery." The magician then glared at Frank. How dare he tell her why she really left!

"Perhaps *you'd* like to join her," Oz said to Frank with a slight undertone of menace to his voice. It was all for show, but then again, Oz was a showman, and a very good one.

Satisfied that he had put Frank back in his place, Oz turned his attention back to May. They had gone over her role before, but he wanted to make sure she knew what to do.

"Now remember, when I ask for a volunteer—" he began.

"I raise my hand," May finished proudly.

Oz gave her a smile. "You are overqualified, my dear."

Turning, he walked out of the trailer, Frank and May close behind. It was time to make some magic.

The show was going smoothly. Oz stood in front of a curtain, crafting a story to go with his tricks. Torches were set up, their flames flickering in the dim light of the tent.

"Journey with me," he began, "across the desert to the mysterious lands of the Arabian Peninsula." In their seats, the audience leaned forward, eager to hear what was to come. Waving his hand, the curtains parted behind him, revealing an Arabian backdrop. People oohed and ahhed. Oz smiled and went on.

Oz motioned with his hands and suddenly the flames on the torches dimmed. The audience gasped. "For five thousand years," Oz continued, "Fernanda's lonely spirit has been trapped. But tonight, we will attempt to free her." Looking out over the audience, Oz suppressed a grin. He had them just where he wanted them. "I will require a volunteer from the audience."

No one raised a hand. Not even May, who sat in the third row looking blankly around.

Oz stifled a groan. "How about *you*, madam?" he finally asked, glaring straight at May.

A look of confusion crossed May's face and then she seemed to remember her job. "Oh! Yes!" she cried. "I'd like to volunteer!"

"How kind of you," Oz said insincerely. He gestured for her to join him on the stage. Turning back to the audience, he began the next part of his act. "A simple country girl, ladies and gentleman!" He looked down at May, who was now standing next to him, her eyes wide. "You have nothing to fear! So long as you *believe*! For when you do believe, *anything* is possible!"

As the audience watched, Oz raised his hand and waved it in front of May, as though controlling an energy that the audience could not see. "Your eyelids grow weary," he intoned. "Grow heavy," he said.

On cue, May's eyelids fluttered and then closed.

"Sleep," Oz ordered sharply. Immediately, May's body grew rigid. "Can you hear me, oh Queen Fernanda?" the Great Oz asked.

"Yes . . ." May hoarsely answered.

The tent filled with an eerie sound and the crowd let out a collective *ooh*, clearly spooked. Oz let the sound reverberate through the tent before he went on. He placed his hand on May's forehead; her body tilted backward, and he said, "Then rise, Fernanda, rise! I *command* you to rise!"

As Oz spoke, May's legs began to come out from under her. And then, she began to float! Noticing that his audience was now well and truly hooked, Oz turned toward a table set up nearby. Sitting on top of the tablecloth was an Arabian urn. In one swift move, Oz pulled the cloth out from under the urn, leaving it undisturbed. Then he gently placed the cloth over May's floating body and lifted his hands in the air. May's body began to rise slowly as sand poured down from the sheet.

"Rise as your spirit flies back to the mystical temple of love in Baghdad," Oz continued.

In the front row, a young girl sat in a wheelchair, her eyes wide with amazement.

She had never seen anything so magical in her entire life. But not everyone was so convinced.

Just as Oz was about to do his big finale, a man cried out, "I see a wire!" He was pointing above May.

Oz paused. He looked first at the man and then over at May's body. The man was right. Light was hitting the stage, illuminating a thin wire. "You are mistaken, sir!" Oz said.

"Am not!" the man shouted. "It's right there!"

Oz puffed out his chest. "A wire?! What need *I* of wires?" He called out to the wings and Frank threw him a sword. SNAP! Whipping the sword back and forth, he cut one of the wires!

The audience gasped as they waited to watch May fall. But she kept floating! Oz cut another wire. SNAP! She *still* kept floating. The tent filled with more gasps. Then Oz whipped the cloth off altogether. May had vanished!

The room erupted in applause. Looking out over the now believers, Oz smiled and threw the cloth at the disbelieving man. Then he bowed deeply. The show was over. Taking one more bow, Oz began to walk off the stage. He wanted to get back to the safety of his trailer while the crowd was still in awe.

But a little voice stopped him.

"Make me walk," the voice said. Turning, Oz saw the little girl in the wheelchair. She was looking up at him with big, hopeful eyes. "Make me walk," she repeated.

Oz didn't know what to do. This had never happened to him before. He turned and tried to catch Frank's eye. Maybe he could help get him out of this jam. But his assistant just raised an eyebrow.

CHAPTER ONE

Leaning down, Oz whispered, "It's just a show, kid."

"But I believe in you," the little girl replied.

Her father came up and stood behind her, his eyes filled with as much hope as his daughter's. Reaching into his pocket, the father pulled out a fistful of crumpled dollar bills. "It's not much," he said, holding the money out. "But it's all we have. Whatever you could do . . ."

The entire tent had gone quiet as people waited to hear what Oz would say. He eyed the money, tempted. But there was no way he could trick himself out of this situation. The girl was in a wheelchair. He could pretend to make May disappear, but he couldn't really make a little girl walk again. While it pained him to turn down money, he had no choice. "I, uh . . ." He struggled with his words. "I would make you walk, but unfortunately, there is distemper in the ether."

As he spoke, hope faded from the girl's eyes. The crowd that had lingered began to boo.

"Beat it, you fake!" one man yelled.

As the boos grew louder, Oz slunk off the stage, struggling to keep his pride.

AS OZ STORMED BACK TO HIS TRAILER, Frank hurried after him, desperately holding on to several magical apparatuses that threatened to fall out of his arms.

"You should have lowered the curtain!" Oz hissed. "I was dying out there!"

"I didn't think it was so bad," Frank said, shrugging. The movement caused the equipment in his arms to shift and he struggled for a moment.

Looking at him out of the corner of his eye, Oz groaned. Of course Frank didn't think it was too bad. He had the intellect of a bedpan. Reaching the trailer, Oz threw open the door and walked inside. He stormed about the small space, taking off his bow tie and throwing his hat in the corner.

CHAPTER TWO

"You know, Professor," Frank said timidly as he watched his boss, "you really shouldn't talk so mean to me all the time. After all, I'm the only friend you've got."

Oz stopped what he was doing and turned to Frank. Then he laughed. "Friend?" he repeated. "You're not my friend, Frank. I don't *need* a friend. What I *need* is someone who knows how to lower a curtain!"

Frank blinked, stung by Oz's harsh words. He opened his mouth, ready to finally stand up for himself, when suddenly there was a knock at his door. Sighing, Frank went to answer it. "It's a woman," he said.

Oz immediately brightened. "Finally!" he said. "Some good news!" Walking over, he peeked out the window. He smiled. The first real, genuine smile he had smiled all day. Throwing open the door, he said, "Hello, Annie."

Standing there was his oldest childhood friend, Annie. She was a beautiful young woman with blond hair and kind eyes. Seeing Oz, she beamed. He pulled her into a hug and for a moment, they just stood there, clearly happy to see one another.

Finally, Oz pulled away and gestured for her to enter. "Don't tell me you just watched that debacle," he said when she was inside.

Annie smiled sadly. "I don't know why you didn't just tell that poor girl the truth," she said in answer.

"What truth?" Oz said, shrugging. "That I'm a fake? They would've had my head! And worse than *that*—demanded a refund!" He paused and then changed the subject. "Can I get you some tea? It's been so long, I haven't seen you since . . ."

"Since the last time you rolled into town," Annie finished, taking a seat. "It's not often enough, Oscar, seeing you once every few months."

"Well, it is a *traveling* circus," he replied, trying to keep the tone light. Annie wasn't like his audiences. He couldn't trick her as easily. "How's the farm?" Oz asked as he made a cup of tea. "And your ma? I've been meaning to write but . . ."

Annie cut him off. "I need to tell you something, Oscar," she said, nervously wringing her hands. Oz stopped pouring the tea and looked over at her. "John Gale asked me to marry him. That's why I've come. I thought you should know."

The trailer grew quiet. Slowly, Oz put down the teapot and stared at it, avoiding Annie's gaze. This was not what he had expected to hear. Annie was Annie. *His* Annie. She had always been *his* Annie. Ever since they were kids on the farm. She had been the only bright thing in his bleak world. Annie and magic were the only things he'd ever really cared about. Still, he knew what he had to say. "Well, I think that's wonderful," he said. "Congratulations."

"I said I had to think about it," Annie said softly.

"Oh, men love that answer," Oz said, trying to mask his true feelings with some levity. But Annie continued on.

"I wondered . . . I wondered what *you* thought I should do."

She looked at Oz, waiting. Her gaze was too much for him, though, and he began to move about the small space, tinkering with a projector and then picking up some glue and rolling the tube in his fingers. He knew what she wanted him to say. He had known for a long time that Annie wanted more than he could give. But it wouldn't be fair to her. She deserved to be happy all the time. Could he really give her that?

"Well, you could do a lot worse than John Gale," he finally said. "He's a good man."

"So are you, Oscar," Annie replied softly.

Oz chuckled. "I am many things, but a good man is not one of them."

Sadness swept over Annie's face. "You could be. If you *wanted* to."

"Well, that's just it," Oz replied, his frustration getting the better of him. "I don't *want* to! Kansas is full of good men. Men who get married and raise families. Men like my father, who spent his whole life tilling the dirt, only to die facedown in it. I don't want that, Annie. I don't want to be a good man. I want to be a *great* man! I want to be Harry Houdini and Thomas Edison all rolled into one." Turning, he flicked a switch and the projector sprang to life. On the far wall an image of an elephant balancing on a ball began to flicker.

Annie sighed. She wished that Oz could see what she saw, that he could believe in himself as much as she did. But he was stubborn. "That's all I ever wanted for you," she finally said. "Greatness." She stood up, ready to leave.

Oz was just about to say something when there was a panicked knock on the door. Frank ducked his head inside.

"Uh, Professor, you need to look outside," he said, nodding over his shoulder.

Going over to the window, Oz pulled aside the small curtain. His eyes grew wide. An angry mob of carnival performers were heading his way—carrying identical music boxes. In the lead was Vlad, the circus's strong man. He was very, *very* angry. Close behind came Vlad's wife and May, followed by many more women.

"Not again!" Oscar groaned. He turned back to Annie. "That's my cue, sweetheart. Congrats on the engagement."

Then, as if their conversation had never happened, he pulled her in for a kiss. It was soft and sweet and for a moment, Oscar wanted to believe he could be the good man Annie wanted. But the angry shouts from outside broke through and he stopped the kiss.

"Oh, Oscar," Annie cried.

"See you in my dreams," he said, just as Vlad burst open the door. Before Annie could say another word, the strong man charged at Oz. Wasting no time, Oz threw his magical cloth over himself and yelled, "Zim Zallah Bim!"

Vlad watched, confused, as the sheet descended to the floor. By the time Vlad and the angry mob rushed over and pulled the curtain off, Oz had disappeared.

Oz was in serious trouble. He could talk or trick his way out of one woman's anger. But a whole mob? And a strong man? That was a different story altogether.

Thankfully he had his trusty trapdoor. Ducking under the curtain, he had been able to open the door and jump down underneath the trailer.

Slipping out from between the wagon wheels, he looked nervously around. The mob was all inside, rallying behind Vlad's angry cries. Seeing his chance, Oz began to run.

Then, a clown spotted him.

"There he is!" the clown cried. Instantly, the group took chase.

Oz ran for his life. He darted between tents and jumped over empty chairs. He turned one corner and around another. And still, the mob kept following. The rest of the carnival workers were busy packing and barely glanced at Oz or Vlad. After all, they were used to seeing strange sights.

As the sky above darkened and the wind began to pick up, Oz ducked around another corner. Pausing to catch his breath, he looked behind him. No one was there! He had lost them. He began to smile, but it faded on his lips as he saw the strong man charge around the corner. Once again he took off, only to run straight into Mr. Baum, the circus owner.

"Oz, where are you going?" Baum asked.

"Mr. Baum, I'll catch up with you in Milwaukee!" Oz yelled as he continued to run.

There was only one way he was going to escape this sticky situation. With the group in hot pursuit, Oz raced straight toward one of the circus's hot-air balloons. It was moored on the outskirts of the carnival, the name OZ emblazoned on its side. As the wind grew even stronger, Oz reached the balloon and quickly shinnied up the mooring rope as Baum looked on.

"You can't keep doing this!" Baum yelled. "That's the third balloon you've stolen from me this year!"

"Take it out of my pay!" Oz quickly replied.

"You don't have any pay!" Baum smartly answered.

With that, Oz heaved himself into the basket, and just in time, too. Vlad and the clown arrived at the rope below and were ready to take Oz down. The big man began to pull on the rope, trying to bring the balloon back down to earth. Scanning the basket, Oz remembered his contraption-knife. He whipped it open to reveal . . . a spoon. Trying again and again, Oz finally found the blade, and began sawing at the rope frantically. Back on the ground, Vlad and the clown kept pulling. For a moment, Oz thought that all hope was lost. And then, with a groan, the rope ripped and the balloon broke free. Vlad and the clown fell backward onto the ground.

At that very moment, Frank arrived. "Oz!" he called out. He was carrying Oz's beloved satchel and hat. "You're gonna need these!"

He hurled the bag up to Oz and then threw the hat like a discus. The objects sliced through the air until Oz reached out and grabbed both . . . just as the balloon lifted higher into the air, pushed up by the wind.

Oz let out a loud laugh. He had done it! He had escaped, once again, relatively unscathed. True, he had had to leave behind a few things, but he would find a way to get them back. And in the meantime, he still had his lovely balloon. Looking down, he gave a big grin and waved to the people on the ground below as they grew smaller and smaller. That had actually been quite a bit of fun. . . .

Only, no one but Frank was waving back. They had all turned and were staring off toward the west. Following their gaze, Oz's eyes grew wide.

"Jiminy Christmas!" he breathed.

On the horizon was the largest, darkest, scariest-looking storm front Oz had ever seen. Angry black clouds churned and a strong wind blew across the flat land, picking up debris and tossing it aside as though it weighed nothing.

And it was coming right at him. . . .

OZ WAS TERRIFIED. Frantically, he began to pull on ropes, desperate to land the balloon, angry mob or not. But the balloon wasn't responding. Looking over his shoulder, Oz's eyes grew wide as terror gripped him. Descending from the dark clouds was the one thing any Kansas native hated to see—an ominous swirling funnel. The storm had become a full-fledged tornado!

"Oh, no!" Oz cried. "No, no, no, no, no!"

Now Oz didn't care about landing, he just wanted to get as far away from the tornado as possible. He cut the sandbags loose and cranked up the burner, hoping to lift the balloon up and over the tornado. But the storm was already upon him.

Winds lashed the basket, whipping Oz's hair into

his eyes and making his skin sting. Lightning flashed and then rain began to pour down. As the tornado moved closer and closer the noise of the howling wind became unbearable. Realizing there was no escape, Oz braced himself just as the tornado blasted into the balloon, sucking it into its funnel.

Darkness swallowed Oz. He was whipped and whirled about as the basket was bashed and battered by the powerful winds. Peering over the basket's edge, Oz's eyes grew even wider. There was a picket fence heading straight toward him. As he watched in horror, several of the fence pickets ripped free and shot right at him. He ducked as the spears flew overhead, narrowly missing him.

The debris kept coming. A mailbox flew by and then a sign shot past. Oz saw grass and dirt and what looked like a stuffed bear. And just when he thought it couldn't get worse, Oz saw his own trailer come swirling up through the funnel. It came right at him, its wood sides missing the balloon by mere inches. Oz let out a sigh of relief. But it was short-lived. The tornado whipped the trailer around, sending it right back at the balloon. There was a loud SMASH as the trailer slammed into the basket and sent the balloon spinning up and over itself. Oz held on for dear life as the balloon spun and spun. Finally, it righted itself. But the danger wasn't over. The basket was falling apart. If it completely broke, Oz would never survive. He let out a cry.

"Please! I don't want to die! I haven't accomplished anything yet!" he screamed into the howling wind. "Get me out of here and I'll do great things!" he yelled.

There was a flash of lightning and then a loud clap of thunder.

"Please give me a chance!" Oz went on. "I promise! I promise I can change!" he pleaded.

Exhausted, Oz slumped down. What was the point? Who would listen to him? More importantly, who would believe him? He wasn't even sure he believed himself.

The balloon continued to spin. Up, up, up it went, climbing toward the top of the tornado. As Oz cowered in the basket, the balloon was launched violently out of the funnel. Then it began to fall—fast. Oz closed his eyes and held on desperately, waiting for the basket to crash to the ground and for his life to be over. Faster and faster it fell . . .

Until . . . everything went quiet.

Oz slowly opened his eyes. The wind had stopped and the howling scream of the twister was gone. Snowflakes drifted down silently, landing on Oz and melting into his suit. Looking up, he saw that the dark clouds were gone, replaced with sunshine and bright blue skies. Gingerly, Oz sat up and peered over the edge of the basket.

He was met with a riot of color. The balloon was floating—miraculously—among tall, oddly-shaped mountains that rose up through bright white clouds. In the distance he could make out more mountains and an endless stretch of blue sky. It was breathtaking. Yet, something about it felt . . . off.

Suddenly, the weather instrument attached to the basket's side stopped and then, after a moment, began spinning in the opposite direction. A moment later, there was a sharp downdraft and the balloon began plummeting down through the clouds. Oz grabbed the edge of the basket. The balloon fell past odd rock formations, narrowly missing one after another. Oz tried to steer but he couldn't. The balloon was out of control. There was a RIIIPPP as the bottom of the basket caught on a sharp cliff edge, and it began to fall faster.

Looking down, Oz felt an odd sense of relief. He

was very close to the ground. If he could just make it a few more feet . . .

SPLASH!

The balloon landed in a rushing river and immediately began to get swept along by the rapids. Oz groaned. Could he just catch a break? First a tornado. Then mountains. Now this? The roar of the river grew louder and Oz turned to look ahead. He gulped. He was definitely *not* catching a break. Up ahead was a huge waterfall!

Before Oz could even scream, the balloon hurtled over the edge of the waterfall. It began to once more plummet to the earth, but then Oz's luck changed. The balloon partially inflated, allowing the basket to softly drop into the water below. Oz let out a cry of joy. He had survived!

He lifted his hands to the sky. "Thank you!" he cried. "Thank you, thank you, thank YOU!"

His screams bounced off the water and suddenly a school of flying fish popped up out of the river. They floated in the air around Oz, staring back at him with eyes that looked almost human. Oz shook his head. He had never seen anything like them before. Where had he landed?

CHAPTER THREE

His wonder quickly turned to panic, though, when he noticed that his basket was sinking. He couldn't swim! Leaping out of the basket, he began to flail about, terror once more rushing through him.

"I can't swim!" he shouted. "Help! I can't sw—!"

Oz's voice trailed off as his foot touched the river's bottom. He was in the shallows! Standing up, he began to laugh at himself. How foolish could he be? Panicking over nothing! Noticing his black hat floating nearby, he bent down to get it. When he stood up, he was no longer alone.

STANDING ON THE SHORE was one of the most beautiful women Oz had ever seen. She was wearing a white shirt, dark pants, and tall riding boots. Over it all she wore a long red jacket. While her clothes were lovely, Oz was more entranced by her big brown eyes, thick, dark hair, and pouty red lips. There was something charming and innocent about her, despite the mischievous glint in her eye.

"Oh, thank goodness!" Oz cried. "I thought I was dead." He paused. "Unless you're an angel. Am I in heaven?" he asked.

The woman shook her head.

"Then there's still hope for me!" Oz cried out, delighted. Looking up at the heavens he added, "You won't regret this."

On the shore, the woman cocked her head, seemingly confused. She looked up at the sky and then back at Oz. "I saw you fall from the sky," she finally said.

Oz nodded. He had thought that was rather obvious. Still, the woman was beautiful. It couldn't hurt to play up the adventure and get a little sympathy. "Yes. My balloon hit an inverted thermal and I couldn't compensate with the . . ."

The woman cut him off. "I'd get out of the water if I were you," she said.

Ah ha! It was already working! "It's actually quite nice," he said, smiling.

"You should be more concerned with the River Fairies, actually," the woman replied, her dark eyes worried. "Their teeth are small but very sharp."

River Fairies? What was she talking about? There were no such things as . . . He let out a yelp as he felt a sharp stab at his ankle. With another cry he began sloshing through the water toward shore. Safely on dry land, Oz looked about. There was something very odd about this place. The trees were so big and the flowers were so bright. It was like nothing he had ever seen before.

"I'm sorry," he said, looking over at the woman. "*Where* am I exactly?"

She smiled at him. "Where do you think you are?"

"I have no idea," Oz replied, shrugging. "It's like no place I've ever seen."

The woman shook her head. "You're in Oz," she said.

Oscar was even more confused. "That's my name," he said, but the woman offered no response. He continued on. "Oscar Zoroaster Phadrig Isaac Norman Henkle Emmanuel Ambroise Diggs!" he said with a tip of his hat. "But everyone calls me Oz." With a flourish, he produced a bouquet of flowers from thin air and handed them to the woman, who became as giddy as a teenager at the gesture.

Immediately, the woman's eyes lit up and she let out a scream of delight. "I knew it!" she cried happily. "The king's prophecy was true."

Suddenly, the woman's face grew serious. "He said that a great wizard bearing the name of our land will descend from the heavens and save us all."

"I don't know about any of that . . ." Oz began. "I'm just trying to get to Milwaukee."

"And here you are. Here to claim your throne," the woman stated.

Oz was confused. "Claim my throne? You mean, like a king's throne?" he asked.

"Well, yes. Because you will be our king," the woman stated very matter-of-factly.

"Your king? Like in a palace, with a crown, and a scepter?" Oz said, starting to hope that this fantasy was true.

"Yes, a beautiful scepter and a grand palace. And you will save all the people!" she exclaimed.

But Oz was already starting to ignore her. "Was that a gold scepter?" he asked.

"Yes. There's more gold than you could ever imagine." Oz's eyes lit up like beacons in the night sky. The beautiful and mysterious woman continued on. "And now Oz will be what it was, because you are the Wizard, aren't you?"

And with the utmost conviction, Oz answered her. "Yes, I am the Wizard," he stated.

But before either of them began to speak there came a loud shrieking from somewhere in the distance. Both Oz and the woman looked up. Silhouetted in the sky were what appeared to be large baboons—with wings.

"What was that?" Oz asked, gulping in fear at the sound from above.

"The Wicked Witch's minions," the woman replied, her voice ominous. "They've been sent to kill you."

"Kill me?" Oz asked nervously. "Wicked Witch? What?" he said, more confused now than ever before.

"We'd better hurry or your reign will be over before it's begun!" the woman said emphatically. Oz didn't know what was going on, but he believed every word she said, so when she raced off into the forest, he immediately followed. After all, he wasn't about to wait around to be killed by some crazy witch's minions.

Oz followed the mystery woman into the dense and lush forest, amazed at the plant life and vegetation that grew all around him. But he didn't have time to dwell on the beauty or the strangeness of the forest—not when they were being chased by flying baboons!

They raced across ravines and down hills. Oz barely had time to register the strange vegetation as he tried not to stumble on the uneven ground. The woman, on the other hand, clearly knew her way in the woods. At one point, she reached back and grabbed his hand, pulling him along as they stepped across a babbling brook. Realizing she was holding his hand, she blushed and pulled away. Up above, a shadow passed by, followed by several more. The Witch's minions had found them again! They had to hide.

"I'm afraid," the woman said.

"So am I," Oz agreed.

Eventually they came to a clearing at the bottom of a majestic waterfall.

Frantically looking around, Oz tried to find someplace safe. Then, looking through the waterfall, he grabbed the woman's hand and began running. There was a ledge he could just make out where they might be able to hide.

Reaching the falls, Oz boosted the woman up onto the ledge and behind the roaring water. He quickly followed.

They huddled behind the water, waiting, as the sound of the baboons faded. Oz turned and glanced at the woman beside him. She really was beautiful. Her cheeks were flushed from the run and her chest rose and fell as she breathed. If it weren't for the whole running-for-their-lives thing, this quiet moment would have been a romantic one.

"Perhaps the Wicked Witch has summoned them back?" she asked hopefully.

"I don't like witches," Oz whispered in reply. The woman smiled. "What's so funny?"

"I too am a witch," she answered. "I'm Theodora the Good."

"You're not a witch," Oz said.

"Of course I am," Theodora said matter-of-factly.

Oz sat up straighter. There was no way this beautiful woman could be a witch! "But . . . where are the warts?" he asked, perplexed. "Where's the broom?"

"What would I do with a broom?" Theodora asked, cocking her head.

"Fly?" Oz replied. He thought it was quite obvious.

But Theodora was baffled. "With a *broom*? I don't understand."

She was clearly not joking. Theodora was a witch. Things were getting stranger and stranger by the minute. "Never mind," Oz said.

But before Oz could continue, a large winged baboon flew down, its nose sniffing the air in front of the falls for a scent of its prey. Oz held his breath. The baboon came closer and closer. Thinking quickly, Oz lifted up his hat and took out a dove. Lifting his hands, the dove flew out from the cave and away from the falls. Seeing the movement, the baboon took off in chase.

Oz slipped off the ledge and turned to help Theodora down. He grabbed her by the waist and lifted her easily. When she was safely on the ground, he moved closer to her, their noses practically touching.

"You were afraid?" she asked, confused at why the all-powerful Wizard would fear the flying baboons.

"Yes," Oz began. "That something would happen to you," he said, clearly masking his fear by turning the conversation back around to her. While she was a witch, Theodora was still just a woman, and he was a master at wooing women—especially beautiful ones.

The words made her heart beat faster and her limbs feel like jelly. Theodora stepped back, confused by these new feelings. As the two walked on through the forest, Theodora couldn't help but steal glances at the man who fell from the sky, and each time she did, a smile crossed her face. She was sure everything was going to work out perfectly.

Z AND THEODORA WALKED through the wondrous land of Oz until they could walk no more. Night had fallen, and the two decided to stop for the night in a clearing. They would head toward the kingdom in the morning.

While camping wasn't his favorite pastime, Oz was willing to spend one night in the woods if he could spend the rest of his nights in a palace. As Oz gathered firewood, he watched as Theodora removed her large red velvet hat. She looked even more beautiful now than ever before, but Oz was still concerned about the events of this afternoon. As the two sat beside the fire, Oz inquired about the Wicked Witch, and just how wicked she really was.

"She's as wicked as they come," Theodora warned. "She poisoned her own father."

"That's pretty wicked," Oz confessed as he stoked the flame.

"He was a good king and a wizard, like you," Theodora explained. "But she wanted the throne all to herself. Poor man." She paused, lost in thought. "But my sister chased her away from the Emerald City."

Oz was impressed. This sister of hers must be quite impressive if she wasn't afraid of a very wicked witch.

"I can't wait for her to meet you!" Theodora went on. "She was starting to doubt you'd ever come. But *now she'll* see! You're going to fix *everything*!"

Silence fell back over the camp as they sat, lost in their thoughts. Oz was worried. He had no idea how to fix his balloon, let alone an entire kingdom.

"You know what I think we need?" Oz eventually said, changing the subject. "A little music."

He reached into his satchel and pulled out one of his infamous music boxes. He wound it up and the lovely tune filled the air. Theodora's face lit up.

"Is it magic?" she asked.

"In a way," Oz answered mysteriously. "It's a music box. Have you never seen one?" She shook her head.

Smiling, he handed it to her. "This belonged to my grandmother, a tsarina from Irkutsk. Here," he said, as he had so many times before. Theodora stared at him in amazement, and his offer turned genuine. "Go on," Oz told her. "I want you to have it."

Theodora hesitated. Slowly, she held out her hand. "No one's ever given me something just because he wanted to."

A part of Oz knew he was playing with fire. After all, while beautiful, Theodora *was* a witch, but he couldn't help himself. "A pretty girl like you? With the visage of Helen of Troy herself? I bet you've had dozens of admirers."

"You don't know much about witches, do you?" Theodora asked with a smile.

"Maybe not, but I'm told I'm a pretty fast learner," Oz said with a similar smile.

Standing up, he extended his hand. "Dance, milady?" Theodora looked at him blankly. "Now you're going to tell me no one's ever danced with you before?"

She shook her head.

"Then it's high time you learned." He pulled Theodora to her feet. Placing his left hand in hers and his right hand on her waist, he pulled her close. She was small next to him, her head barely coming to his chin. "Now just try to feel the music," Oz said softly.

Slowly, they began to dance. As they moved around the camp, fireflies came out, their bodies illuminating the area and making everything sparkle. Theodora's heart raced. She had never felt like this before. She felt as though she were floating. Cautiously, she placed her head on his chest.

"Nice, isn't it?" Oz said softly. "You like it?"

Theodora tilted her head up and nodded, her eyes full of wonder. "Yes."

Oz smiled gently. He knew that look. He had seen it many times before. His music box had worked its magic once again. As the music continued to play and the fireflies fluttered in the dark, Oz pulled Theodora closer and then, ever so gently, pressed his lips to hers. . . .

The next morning dawned brightly, the sunshine making Oz's good mood even better. He had had a lovely evening and now he and Theodora were on their way to *his* kingdom. It was utterly perfect.

As they continued to walk along, Oz whistled a

happy little tune. In front of them, a beautiful butterfly emerged from its cocoon and flitted over to settle on Theodora's finger. The music died on Oz's lips though when he looked down and saw Theodora staring up at him. She was gazing at him tenderly.

As they continued to walk along, she would smile up at him happily, and every once in a while she would even skip.

"It's incredible," she said at one point. "Here I thought I'd live a lonely life, and then you showed up. Not only are you the Wizard, you're the person I belong with."

Oz gulped. Okay, this was getting a little out of control. "Well, we sure get along. . . ." he said.

"And?" Theodora asked, probing. Clearly she wanted more.

"And . . . like *you* said, we belong together?" he went on, unsure.

Theodora smiled. She was about to go on when a loud shriek pierced the air. Quickly, Oz pulled Theodora off the main path. He didn't want to get caught by any of those huge baboons.

"Help me!" a voice shouted from close behind them. "Somebody save me!"

Chapter Five

Turning, Oz and Theodora saw a small monkey. The creature was dressed in what appeared to be a bellhop uniform and was struggling to untangle himself from a long vine.

"Oh!" Theodora said. "That poor little creature! Wizard, we must save him!"

Oz looked at her and then back at the monkey. Was she serious? Why did he need to save a monkey? After all, it was probably this little guy's big cousins that had come after him earlier. But Theodora wouldn't take no for an answer. She shoved Oz toward the monkey.

Leaning down, Oz took a closer look at the vines. They were well and truly wrapped tight. He began to tug at the vines. "Of course I can save this little talking monkey in a bellhop's uniform," he muttered under his breath.

"Please, hurry up!" the monkey begged. "Do you have anything sharp? Like a knife or something? How about your teeth? What kind of teeth you got?"

The monkey was making Oz nervous. "Calm down," he said, pulling out his pocket knife. "It's going to be all right."

But the monkey was not getting any calmer. In

fact, he seemed to be getting more and more scared by the minute. "You gotta get me out of these vines," he cried. "I'm going to die! It's going to eat me!"

Well, Oz thought, that was just ridiculous. "Don't worry. These vines aren't going to eat you," he said, still trying to calm the monkey down.

But the creature shook his head. "Not the vines! The lion!"

"Lion?" Oz repeated.

As if on cue, there was a deafening roar. Turning, Oz saw a giant lion standing on a nearby rock. "Eat him first! Eat him first!" the monkey yelled to the lion.

The king of the jungle opened its jaws and let out another roar. Oz began to shake as hard as the monkey.

Then . . . the lion charged!

Oz didn't have much time. The lion was almost upon them. Thinking quickly, he reached into his pocket and pulled out a handful of smoke pellets. He threw them. As they hit the ground in front of the lion they exploded, sending red smoke billowing into the air. Seeing the smoke, the lion panicked and ran.

"Zim Zallah Bim! Be gone, coward! Fear my greatness!" Oz yelled in an overly dramatic fashion as the lion disappeared into the forest.

"You were wonderful, Wizard," Theodora said when they were safe.

The monkey, who had pulled himself out of the vines, looked up at Oz and cocked his head. "Wizard? You mean the prophecy was true?" he asked.

Theodora nodded happily while Oz shrugged. "All right, well, saved the day," he said. "Just a little prestidigitatic display. Shall we go to the palace now?"

With a nod from Theodora, the pair turned and began to walk away. "Wait!" the monkey called out. "Please, sir! My name is Finley. My master's home was ransacked by the Wicked Witch's baboons and I've been hiding in these woods ever since." He stopped and raised his hand to the sky. "You've saved my life, o Wizard. So I hereby swear a life debt to you."

"No need," Oz said, waving Finley off.

But Finley would not take no for an answer. "From this moment on, I shall be your loyal and faithful servant until death."

Oz sighed. He didn't really need a loyal or faithful servant. He imagined there would be plenty of those at the palace. Still, Theodora was looking up at him pleadingly. "Well, he is cute. . . ." she said.

Oz was convinced. "All right, you're hired," he said.

"Wonderful," Finley said. "Let's shake on it."

But instead of shaking, Oz held out his bag. "My bag, Monkey."

"With pleasure," Finley said. But when Oz handed him the bag, the weight of it caused him to plummet to the ground. He struggled to get up. "I got it! You two run along!"

A short while later, they rounded a corner and Oz stopped in his tracks. At the end of the road was a huge glimmering city. Its radiant green towers and turrets soared into the sky, spanning the horizon.

"The Emerald City," Theodora explained. "Just down this hill and along the Yellow Brick Road. Just think, it will all be yours now."

Taking in the vista, Oz smiled broadly. This would do quite nicely. "It's a good thing green is my favorite color," he said, laughing.

Theodora looked up at him, pleased. "You're going to make the best king Oz has ever known," she said. "And I'll be so proud to be . . . your queen."

Oz stopped smiling. Then he blinked. "My queen?" he repeated.

"Of course," Theodora replied. "We'll spend a

lifetime together. Right now there are thousands of people in Oz waiting to witness your miracles!" Letting out a giddy little squeal of joy she reached up and gave him a kiss. Then, turning, she ran off down the hill.

Thousands? That was quite a lot of people. The biggest show he would ever have done . . . Could he handle it?

"What now, Wizard?" the small flying monkey asked.

Noticing Finley, Oz turned to him. "Monkey," he said as they began to follow Theodora down the hill. "Tell me again about that life debt?"

Proudly, Finley explained. "I devote my life to you. Whatever you wish, whatever you want, it's my sworn duty to deliver for you until the end of my days."

"And there's no getting out of it?" Oz asked.

Finley nodded. "None, sir. It is irrevocable."

"Good," Oz said. "Because I'm not the Wizard." He didn't know why, but he had felt the need to tell someone the truth. And if the monkey was in debt to him, he could never tell anyone the truth . . .

Finley let out a laugh. "Oh, sir. Your sense of humor is as boundless as it is wondrous. You remind me—"

"I'm not the Wizard," Oz repeated.

For a moment, the monkey didn't say anything as he tried to process Oz's words. Then, when he realized the man wasn't kidding, his eyes grew wide. "But you could have told me before I sealed the life debt!" he complained. "You gotta come clean for that innocent young girl."

Oz nodded. "I'll deal with her later," he said. "As my new assistant, all you need to know are the three ups: show up, keep up, shut up."

"But I . . ." Finley began.

Oz held up a finger. "What's the third up?"

Finley scowled.

"Right," Oz went on. "Now listen, I'm depending on you. We need to convince the good people of Oz that they found their Wizard."

Before Oz could go on, he saw that they had caught up with Theodora. She was standing in front of a line of very, very tall men wearing uniforms. These were the Winkie Guards who protected the Emerald City. And standing in front of them was a small man with a very sour expression. Nearby was a jewel-encrusted carriage being pulled by two snow-white horses.

"Theodora," the little man said, "we've been expecting you."

"Hello, Knuck," Theodora said. "*This* is the Wizard."

"How do you do, sir?" Oz said as he extended his hand. But the small man just continued to stare at him.

"This is the Wizard?" Knuck said, not wanting to believe his own eyes.

The Munchkin's reaction immediately put Oz on the defensive. "Is there a problem?" Oz asked.

Knuck looked Oz up and down skeptically. "Yeah. I thought you'd be taller."

Oz forced himself not to laugh. This coming from a guy who barely came up to his belt?

Turning back to the Winkies, Knuck raised a large staff. "All hail the Wizard!"

"ALL HAIL THE WIZARD!" the Winkies cried.

Beside Oz, Finley raised an eyebrow. "All hail the Wizard! The mightiest of the mighties!" he hissed under his breath. "The greatest, most powerful and most *genuine* of real and true wizards."

Oz shot the monkey a glare. Enough was enough, but the monkey just kept going. "A Wizard above scrutiny, with no covert agenda or subversive intention whatsoever. A Wizard of the highest moral rectitude. He's just a real, good, solid Wizard, everyone." Oz finally caught Finley's eye, and the monkey finished his rant. "The Wizard," he said. "Here he is."

Ignoring him, Oz followed Knuck, who opened the door to the carriage and ushered Oz inside. It was time for Oz to see inside the Emerald City.

THE EMERALD CITY had once been a magnificent place. Towers, spires, and fountains dominated the skyline, everything the same shade of green. But when Oz got closer, it was clear that the city had fallen upon hard times. The towers were crumbling and shop windows were broken. On one wall, ominous claw marks could be made out, causing Oz to shudder.

He shook his head. It was all just cosmetic. A few coats of paint and some new windows and the place would look good as new.

"The kingdom needs a little sprucing up!" Oz said. He would make this his first order of business.

Theodora saw the confusion in Oz's eyes and put

a gentle hand on his. "The Wicked Witch sends her baboons on nightly raids," she explained. "My sister has set up sentries along the wall, but there's only so much they can do. Things will be different now that you are here."

As they moved down the road, however, Oz noticed something, well, off about the people as well. No one looked particularly happy. They passed a woman hanging laundry, her shoulders slumped. A bricklayer repaired a wall, his face drawn. When the carriage moved by a young boy and his mother, both of whom were filled with fear, the mother called out to him. "Help us, Wizard!" she begged. "Please!"

The Winkie Guard pushed the woman aside so that the carriage could continue on through. Then a ragged old man yelled directly at Oscar. "Save us from the Wicked Witch!" he pleaded.

Oz didn't understand. What was going on? Why were these people so desperate for help? Shouldn't these people be happy? Theodora had told him they would cheer when they saw him, as he was their savior. This behavior was decidedly *unexcited*.

"Don't worry," Theodora said, trying to reassure Oz. "Things'll be different now that you're here."

CHAPTER SIX

But Oz had no more time to ponder the strange behavior of the people. The carriage had reached the palace. Unlike the rest of the city, the palace was in pristine shape. It glittered and sparkled in the sunlight and seemed to go on forever. Pleased, Oz got out of the carriage and followed Theodora inside and down a long vaulted corridor. At the end stood a set of tall double doors that opened all by themselves when they approached.

Oz's eyes grew wide. Behind the doors was the most opulent room he had ever seen. It was a large chamber, decorated in green, with huge windows that looked out upon the city. The floor beneath his feet was made of green marble and covered with an intricate design. Hanging above them were huge chandeliers, their soft light casting warm shadows on the walls. At the far end of the room, a short flight of stairs led up to a huge emerald throne.

"Is that it?" Oz asked. "Is that my throne?"

But it was not Theodora who answered. From behind him, a voice responded, "Do you like it?"

Turning, Oz found himself looking at a stunning woman. She appeared to be a bit older than Theodora, but with the same dark hair and ruby lips. But while

Theodora's eyes were full of innocence, this woman's were penetrating, as though she knew more than she was willing to let on. Smiling, she looked Oz up and down as she brought a hand to her throat and touched the large emerald jewel that hung around her neck.

"I've personally kept watch over it," the woman went on, "waiting for your arrival."

"Much obliged," Oz said, tipping his head and giving her one of his most charming smiles.

The woman responded in kind. "Praise be you're here at last, and the prophecy shall be fulfilled. This is a glorious day for us all." Then the woman gave Oz a charming smile. "And may I add," the woman said with an extra glint in her eye, "you are as handsome a king as we've ever had."

"Flatterer," Oz said as he turned back toward Theodora. "Who is this fetching woman?"

Theodora stepped up, placing herself by Oz's side. "Wizard," she said, "this is my sister."

"I am Evanora, the royal advisor," the woman added. "I have protected the Emerald City whilst we awaited your arrival. I am here to serve you as I have served the king before you."

Oz waggled an eyebrow. "I look forward to being served," he said, his voice teasing.

Evanora flashed a wicked smile. "Oh, sister," she began, "I like him already."

As Theodora glanced jealously between the two of them, Oz bounded up the stairs and took a seat on the throne.

The smile on Evanora's face faltered briefly. But before Oz could notice, she forced a new one. "Yes, have a seat. How does it feel?"

"Fits like a glove!" Oz exclaimed.

"Knuck will show you to your quarters. We'll chat more later?" Evanora asked.

"Can't wait!" Oz exclaimed. He was like a kid in a candy store. Spotting Finley, he called out to his newfound friend. "Monkey, my bag!" he barked.

"Yes, Wizard," Finley said as he grabbed Oz's bag. "Right away, oh great and powerful one," he said with a hint of sarcasm that went undetected by the sisters, but not by Oz, who quickly ushered the monkey out and followed him close behind.

When they were alone, Theodora turned to her sister, giddy. "Isn't he wonderful! Didn't I say he would come?" But her sister didn't agree.

Evanora's features hardened and the smile completely

vanished from her face. She was not pleased. Not pleased at all. What was her sister *thinking*? Theodora had always been the young and impulsive one, but this was pure madness.

"You dare escort that oaf in here!" Evanora spat. "Allow him to climb into that hallowed throne—"

"And why not? He *is* the Wizard," Theodora protested.

Evanora scoffed. "Or so he *says*! Did it not occur to you that he might be an impostor, in league with the Wicked Witch? Sent here to *kill* us?"

"The Wicked Witch?" Theodora repeated. "Don't be ridiculous."

Evanora raised a sculpted eyebrow. "*I'm* not the one underestimating her cleverness," she pointed out. "Or maybe it's you I'm underestimating. Have you finally joined her side, sister?"

"Do you honestly think I could conspire against you? With *her*?" Theodora protested. "You're my sister, Evanora, and I love you. But we must all step back and allow fate to take its course," she said as she took her sister's hand and looked into her eyes.

"You're right," Evanora agreed. "But I want proof that he is who he claims to be," she said.

CHAPTER SIX

"He's already proven hims—" Theodora began, but Evanora was quick to cut her off.

"Not to me he hasn't," she stated.

Theodora let her sister's words hang in the air as she considered them. "Very well," she said.

Satisfied, Theodora pulled her sister to the side and led her out of the throne room. "I just need to give him one little test," she said as the two disappeared down the long green hallway.

HIGH ABOVE THE CITY, Oz found himself following Evanora across a narrow footbridge. He had been surprised when the older sister had offered to give him a tour of the palace, but he had quickly agreed. After all, it *was* his palace now, and it was truly magnificent.

"Thank you for the tour," Oz said as they walked along.

"It's my job," Evanora replied with a slight bow of her head.

"Giving tours?" Oz said, amused.

"Taking care of the king," Evanora replied.

"Well, then," Oz began, with a new gleam in his eye. "You know, I was thinking: a royal feast might be—"

"My sister tells me your magic is quite powerful," Evanora said, stopping Oz dead in his tracks.

"Really?" Oz said, surprised. Catching himself, he went on. "I mean . . . yes, of course. Boggling to the minds of all who witness it."

Evanora looked back and gave him a charming smile. "I can't wait to see for myself. Why not show me now?"

"All things in good time," he hedged. "And a good time for all things!"

They continued making their way along the footbridge. At the other end was a large one-room turret. A gust of wind shook the bridge slightly and Oz looked down. He gulped. They were very, *very* high.

"There's one last room I want you to see," Evanora said, oblivious to Oz's nerves.

Dragging his gaze from the dizzying heights, he saw that the older witch had opened the turret's doors. His breath caught in his throat. The room sparkled and shone with thousands upon thousands of pieces of treasure. Gemstones of every color sat among chests full of gleaming gold coins. A large statue of a winged horse glimmered, its body made of solid gold, and nearby was a vase covered in intricate artwork. The treasure filled every nook and cranny of the room, completely covering the floor and rising up against the walls. This was the Room of Resplendence.

"The Royal Treasure of Oz," Evanora explained. "It belongs to whoever is king."

Oz's eyes rolled back. He swooned, then looked back at Evanora. "It's all right, Wizard," she said. "Go and enjoy your riches!" That was all Oz needed to hear.

As Evanora watched, Oz seemed to faint, hitting the treasure-covered ground with a thud. He lay still for a moment and then he began moving his arms up and down, making angels in the coins just like a giddy little schoolboy.

"It's mine!" he shouted with glee. "Mine! No more secondhand suits! Nothin' but silks and satins and—" He reached down and picked up a gold cup. "A chalice! I always wanted a chalice! And now I've got one!"

"Well, not quite yet," Evanora said. Oz stopped rolling around in the gold and looked up at her quizzically. She went on. "You only become king *after* you defeat the Wicked Witch. *That's* the prophecy. And since you haven't done that yet . . ."

". . . I'm not actually king?" Oz finished.

Evanora nodded. "Not yet, no. You still have to defeat the Wicked Witch. And killing her . . . won't be easy."

"No, I can't imagine it would b—" He paused. "Now wait a minute! Nobody mentioned *killing* anyone!" Defeating and killing were two very different things. He had thought maybe he would have to give her a firm talking-to. But killing? That was a little, well, violent, for his tastes.

Evanora frowned. "Oh, well," she said, her tone stern. "If you're not interested in being king, that's all right with me. We can just forget about the whole thing. The gold, the rubies, the chalice . . ."

"But I *am* interested!" Oz cried. "I'm just not too keen on killing a lady."

"She's a wicked *witch*!" Evanora clarified. "And your magic is the only thing strong enough to destroy her. All you have to do is journey to the Dark Forest and destroy her wand." She looked into his eyes, begging him silently.

"Her wand?" Oz inquired.

"Yes, it's the source of all her power," Evanora informed him. "Without it, she dies."

"Uh, I haven't even said good-bye to Theodora.

She will be upset," Oz said, trying to buy himself some more time.

"I will talk to her in the morning," Evanora said. "I will tell her how much you love her, how much you—"

"No," Oz quickly interrupted. "No, don't say anything."

"All right. I will say whatever it is you want me to say, but, are you going to save us all, or not?" Evanora asked with all sincerity, her eyes locked on his.

Oz sighed and tried to muster a smile. He had no choice. He wanted the kingdom. No matter what the cost. It looked like he was going to go on his very own witch hunt.

***

Once again, Oz found himself walking along the Yellow Brick Road. This time, though, his only companion was the surly flying monkey. As the Emerald City faded into the distance behind them, Oz turned to Finley. The monkey let out a troubled sigh. "We really going to do this?" Finley asked.

"How hard can it be to kill a wicked witch?" Oz asked.

Finley narrowed his eyes. "Hard," he began.

"Really hard. It's very, very hard to kill a wicked witch. And what about that poor girl back there? I think she really liked you," he said, referring to Oz's relationship with Theodora.

"She'll get over me. They always do," Oz said. He had been through this plenty of times before back in Kansas. "She's a pretty young witch; plenty of wizards will be knocking at her door."

Finley shook his head. "Every lie you tell gets us one step closer to the Emerald City dungeon," he said.

"Then don't think of them as lies, think of them as stepping stones on the road to greatness!" Oz said, completely believing his own fibs and fabrications. But Finley wasn't buying it.

"Wait! I've got it!" the flying monkey began. "We'll turn around and go back. You'll come clean. You apologize for lying about being the Wizard and for lying to that poor girl. Okay?" Oz glared at him, but Finley was just getting started. "You gotta really seem contrite, you gotta sell it," the flying monkey continued. "Maybe you can even cry. Can you cry? I could cut up an onion."

"We're not going back," Oz said with a marked confidence. "We're going to find this Wicked Witch, and I'm going to steal her wand. I'll get that big pile of gold, and you can have a nice pile of bananas, all right?"

Dumbfounded, Finley dropped Oz's bag. "Bananas?" he asked, as he gave Oz a long, cold stare. "Oh, I see," the monkey began. "Because I'm a monkey? I must love bananas, right? That is a vicious stereotype!" the monkey exclaimed.

"You don't like bananas?" Oz asked.

"No, of course I love them. I'm a monkey; don't be ridiculous," Finley said. "I just don't like you saying it. How about this—we offer to wash all the windows in the Emerald City for an entire year. They'd have to forgive us, right? Or we can give them a little help with their infrastructure. I noticed some yellow-brick potholes back there," the monkey pleaded. But Oz just stared at him blankly.

An awkward silence fell over the pair as they continued to walk down the road. It was going to be a very long, very uncomfortable, journey. . . .

A short while later, Oz and Finley crested a small hill. Looking ahead, Oz noticed several plumes of smoke rising from just over the next hill. "That looks bad," Finley said, his voice now full of concern.

"We're not going down there," Oz stated. It was bad enough he had to find and defeat a wicked witch, he wasn't about to investigate a possible fire.

"But someone might need our help!" Finley said as he flew toward the smoke.

Oz was suddenly a bundle of nerves. "Get back here!" he yelled to Finley. "You get back here! Are you trying to get us killed to get out of this life debt? We've got to get the Wicked Witch. What are we doing over here?" But Finley didn't answer. He just continued on toward the plumes of smoke. Oz realized that he once again had no choice. His pace quickened as he left the Yellow Brick Road and followed Finley down toward the smoke.

As they reached the bowl of the valley, the ground under their feet began to change. The grass grew stiffer, and then it began to crunch and clink. Looking down, Oz saw that the grass seemed to be made of glass. In fact, the rocks, trees, even the flowers all looked smooth and shiny, reminding Oz of his great-aunt's china collection. But it wasn't just the grass, it was the entire town. There were barns and farms and streets just like a regular town—only everything was made entirely of china!

Making their way into the center of the village,

Oz's heart began to beat nervously. Something terrible had happened here. Everywhere he looked, china was broken and smashed, strewn about as if a giant hand had reached down and smashed the village.

Bending over to pick up a hunk of china, Oz recoiled. A porcelain face stared back at him. Looking around, he began to pick out more faces among the heaps of broken china. A wave of sadness swept over Oz. Who could have done such a thing? Clearly, this was once a living and breathing place. Now it was just a wasteland.

From the ruins of a nearby house came the sound of crying. Oz exchanged a look with Finley. It was a dangerous situation, but they both knew they had to investigate the crying sound. Then in the distance came the shrieks of the flying baboons. They sounded like they were coming straight toward them!

He and Finley ran into the house, jumping over mounds of shattered porcelain and entering what had once been a parlor. There, sitting on the floor, was a beautiful little china girl. She had white china hair, big sad eyes, and she was wearing a white and blue dress.

"Hey there," Oz called out. "Are you all right?"

The girl looked up, still crying. Seeing Oz and Finley, she recoiled in fear.

"It's okay, we won't hurt you," Oz said, his voice gentle. Carefully, he made his way closer to the girl. He nodded at the monkey. "This is Finley. And my name is Oz."

The little girl's eyes grew wide. "Are you . . . are you the Wizard?" she stammered.

"You've heard of me?" Oz asked, surprised. She nodded. Apparently news traveled fast in this land. "Then you have nothing to be afraid of. Now come on out of there."

"But I can't," the little girl replied. She looked down at her legs. For the first time, Oz noticed that they were broken off in several places. "I'll never get back together," she said with a catch in her throat.

Oz flashed back to his last show in Kansas and the little girl begging for his help. He hadn't been able to do anything then—what were the chances he could do something now? He racked his brain, trying to think of a solution, and then it hit him. "Don't worry, I think I have something!" he said. After ordering Finley to toss him his satchel, Oz began to rummage through it. With a cry of triumph, he pulled out a bottle of quick-drying glue. "Here it is!" Oz said in triumph. But China Girl was confused.

"What is it?" she asked.

"Magic in a bottle," Oz said with a smile. "Let's give it a try!"

The girl's eyes widened in amazement as Oz began to gather up the pieces of her broken legs. One by one he started gluing them together. As he worked, the shrieks of the baboons grew louder and closer.

"Oh, no! They're coming back!" China Girl exclaimed. Oz quickly gathered her and Finley into a tight huddle. A dark shadow passed outside as the creatures flew over the house and then continued on their way. Oz let out the breath he hadn't realized he'd been holding.

"The Witch sent them," China Girl explained. "The whole town was celebrating, out in the streets, because we had heard that you'd finally arrived."

The little girl continued her tale. She told them how everyone was so happy and they couldn't help but make noise. That they kept cheering, right up until the Witch's baboons came in and began to destroy everything. As she spoke, the little girl's eyes welled up with tears.

Oz listened, feeling a strange sense of guilt. His arrival had caused all this destruction, all this loss. Shaking his head, he glued the last piece of the girl's leg. "Would you like to stand?" he asked, smiling weakly.

Nodding, the little girl mustered up all her strength and heaved herself into a standing position. A huge smile spread across her face.

"Now walk to me," Oz said. But China Girl was afraid. She didn't want to break her legs again.

"I don't think I can," she said.

"I think you can," Oz said as he looked into her eyes. "Come on."

China Girl steeled herself as Oz held his breath. Tentatively, she moved her foot forward, taking a small step. Then she took another. And another. Soon, she was walking all around the room.

Oz burst into laughter. He had done it! Reaching him, China Girl fell into his arms, overjoyed. Oz was surprised at the outpouring of emotion, and the fact that he, too, felt an overwhelming sense of both pride and hope. He turned to look at Finley, but the flying monkey had already looked away. He was trying to conceal the tear in his eye. The last thing he wanted was for Oz to see him crying.

O Z'S GOOD FEELINGS were replaced with guilt when he tried to send China Girl back to the Emerald City. Even though it would be safer behind the city's walls, the little girl wanted none of it. She wanted to help Oz.

"On a witch hunt?" Oz asked. "No," he said. "You're just a little girl."

"I'm not as delicate as I look," China Girl said. And with that, she ran over and kicked Oz in the shins.

"That didn't hurt," Oz said, even though it did. But the girl wouldn't budge.

"Look," Oz began. "We have one rule in show-biz. Never work with kids or animals," he said as he glanced over at Finley. Then he turned back to her. "The answer is no," he said with grim determination. But Oz wasn't prepared for what came next.

China Girl looked up at him and her eyes filled with big tears. Then her lower lip began to quiver. Before Oz knew what was happening, she was in hysterics. "You're going to leave me alone? On a road? In the middle of nowhere?"

Oz was a goner.

China Girl continued to cry and cry until Oz could take no more. "Fine!" he yelled. "Fine! You wanna come? Come! We'll all go! It'll be a big party!" he said as he threw his arms in the air, exasperated.

And with that, China Girl immediately stopped her crying. "Great! Let's go kill ourselves a witch!" she said as she skipped down the Yellow Brick Road.

Oz shot Finley a look of utter disbelief. "I think I just got conned," the con man said to the monkey.

"Yeah? How does it feel?" Finley asked. The two just stared at each other. This little girl was quite possibly smarter than both of them.

⚜

Oz now found himself back on the Yellow Brick Road with a flying monkey and a girl made of china. And they were on their way to kill a witch.

The china village quickly faded behind them, and soon they found themselves in a dark forest. Bats fluttered past as they made their way deeper and deeper into the trees. From high in a tree, a crow as black as night cawed a warning to them that they would not make it out of the woods alive. This gave everyone the creeps, but no one more than China Girl, who lifted her arms up to Oz so she could be carried. Oz obliged and picked her up, only to notice Finley with his arms raised and a "pick me up too" look on his face. Oz just rolled his eyes and the trio kept moving.

"This is terrifying, but at least there are no spiders," Finley said. "I hate spiders," the monkey admitted. The place was giving him the spooks. And he wasn't alone.

"Do you think there are ghosts out here?" China Girl asked.

"No, of course not," Oz responded, trying to convince both her and himself that there weren't any.

"Evil spirits, maybe? The undead?" she countered.

"The und—? Would you stop that!" Oz yelled. He didn't think he could be more afraid—until a glowing snapdragon-like flower lunged from the forest at them, causing them all to scream. More and more of the odd snapdragon flowers attacked, causing Oz, China Girl, and Finley to weave and dodge out of their way . . . and run!

Rounding a corner, the trio was able to slow down and catch their breath. "Oh my gosh, that was close!" China Girl said. But before she could continue, something caught her eye. "Where are we?" she asked, and when Oz and Finley turned to look, they grew even more frightened. There, in front of them, was a rusty fence. And behind the fence was a sea of gravestones set amid bent and gnarled trees.

"This must be the place," Oz muttered under his breath.

"So how you gonna kill the Witch?" China Girl asked when they reached the graveyard's edge. Unlike Oz, she seemed to be enjoying the idea.

"All I need to do is get a hold of her wand," Oz said grumpily. At least that was what Evanora had told him before she sent him off. "Once I destroy that, she's finished."

"Why don't you just use this?" she asked, pulling out a large knife.

"Hey!" Oz cried, taking a step back. "Where'd you get that?!"

The girl shrugged. "I'm made of china," she said matter-of-factly. "I've got to protect myself somehow."

"Give me that! Honestly!" Oz yelled. This was out

of control. Not only was he supposed to be killing a witch, he had a knife-carrying girl made of china trying to help. It was beyond absurd. If he weren't so scared, he might have even laughed. But he didn't. Instead, he grabbed the knife.

"Honestly yourself," China Girl muttered. Then something appeared that caught their attention.

At the edge of cemetery, a lone figure in a long black cloak appeared through the thick fog. All three of them ducked behind a nearby boulder. Carefully, they peered over the edge. The Witch was literally floating through the air. As they watched, she landed next to the cemetery gate and pulled a basket from her cloak. Then she bent down to pick some flowers. As she worked, she placed her wand on a broken-down cart nearby, unaware that she was being watched. Oz shivered.

"That must be her," China Girl said.

"She put down the wand," Oz replied, sure that this was the Wicked Witch that he had to defeat.

"But how are you going to get it?" China Girl asked.

He racked his brain, trying to figure out a plan. Then it hit him! In magic, the most important element was misdirection. If the magician could get the audience to look *that* way while he did something *this* way, they were never aware of the sleight of hand, and the trick was a success. All he needed was some misdirection! Grabbing a tool from his satchel, he began to draw in the dirt.

"Now listen up. Here's the plan," he told the others when he was done. In front of him was a crudely drawn map of the graveyard with various symbols on it. "This triangle is the Witch. Monkey, you're the 'X.' I'm the 'O,' and China Girl, you're the squiggly line."

"I want to be a heart," China Girl said, pouting. "Can I be a heart?"

Oz stifled a groan. "Fine," he said. "You're a heart. Heart stays here. X moves there. O moves toward triangle, like this." As he spoke, he pointed to the various symbols and indicated where they should go. When he was done, he looked at Finley. "Well?"

Finley leaned down closer to the dirt. He scrunched his eyes and then his nose began to twitch. And then . . . he sneezed!

"Good work. You just sneezed away the plan!" Oz cried under his breath.

"I'm sorry," Finley said. "Now, was I the triangle or the heart?"

Oz didn't have time to draw up a new plan and explain it. So instead, he told Finley to fly up into a nearby tree. When he gave the signal, Finley would start making animal noises and Oz would use the distraction to steal the wand.

With a nod, Finley flew into the branches. Then it was Oz's turn. Taking a deep breath, he crept out from behind the boulder. His heart was racing. He had no idea what he was doing.

By that point, he had almost reached the cart. He reached out a hand, ready to grab the wand, and . . .

"MOOOOOOOOOOO!"

Oz ducked down just as the Witch whipped around to see where the strange cow sound was coming from. Crouched behind the cart, Oz slapped his forehead. A cow? Finley was imitating a cow? What was that crazy monkey thinking?

But . . . it was working!

As Finley kept mooing, the Wicked Witch turned again so that her back was now toward Oz. It was his chance! Reaching forward, he snatched the wand from the cart and hightailed it back to China Girl.

"I got it!" Oz exclaimed.

"Break it!" yelled Finley.

The small-town citizens of Kansas are eager to be entertained by the BAUM BROS. CIRCUS.

A WHIRLING TORNADO whisks Oz and his hot air balloon away from Kansas.

Oz flies toward the beautiful and wondrous LAND OF OZ.

After splashing down into a rushing river, Oz is greeted by THEODORA THE GOOD.

Oz and Theodora get better acquainted.

Theodora shows Oz the sparkling Emerald City.

Oz tries out his new golden throne in the EMERALD CITY.

Finley and Oz make their way into the damaged CHINA TOWN.

EVANORA, bent on destruction, releases the flying baboons!

Glinda and Oz travel by bubble to her castle in **QUADLING COUNTRY**.

THE WICKED WITCHES scheme to attack Oz and Glinda, and overtake the land.

OZ AND THE TINKERS prepare for their upcoming battle against the Wicked Witches.

The Wicked Witches capture GLINDA THE GOOD!

OZ shows the Land of Oz how powerful he truly is.

GLINDA FIGHTS the Wicked Witch for the good people of Oz.

OZ AND GLINDA celebrate their victory against the Wicked Witches.

CHAPTER EIGHT

"Break it, Wizard! Break it!" echoed China Girl.

For a moment, Oz just looked at the wand. It didn't seem particularly dangerous. It almost seemed like a toy. But, rules were rules. He had to destroy the Wicked Witch if he wanted the kingdom and to destroy the Witch he had to destroy the wand. He lifted it over his head and began to bend it down on each side when the Witch spoke.

"Are you really the Wizard?" the shrouded figure asked.

Oz wasn't expecting her to talk, or for her voice to sound so delicate. The man from Kansas was caught completely off guard, and was still completely terrified. "Well, that's a com—complicated question. I mean, what is a wizard?" Oz stammered.

Before Oz could go on, the Witch stepped forward and pulled off her hood. Oz's breath caught in his throat. She was stunning. Her hair was long and so blond it almost appeared silver, and her eyes were warm and kind. She looked so familiar, so much like Annie, that for a moment, Oz was speechless. Then, he found his voice.

"Yes," he said, seeing a chance to impress another beautiful woman. "I'm the Wizard."

The blond woman's eyes welled with tears as she smiled at him. "Then there's hope," she said, sounding relieved.

China Girl looked to Finley, confused. "What's going on?" she whispered.

"I don't know," the monkey replied. "I sneezed the plan away."

"I've waited so long to meet you," the beautiful Witch said to Oz.

"So . . . we've never met?" he asked, thinking of Annie.

The Witch shook her head. "Certainly not," she said in a soft, gentle voice. "I would've remembered a thing like that," she said with a soft smile.

But Oz was still staring at her in disbelief. "You've never been to Kansas?" he asked.

"What is Kansas?" the Witch asked. "Is that where you're from? Oh my, you must have traveled very far to get to the land of Oz," she said. Then, after a pause, she said, "I am Glinda the Good, the Witch of the South."

"So, you're the good witch?" Oz asked, once again confused. "I thought Evanora was the good witch." Oz raised an eyebrow. Good witch? Wicked witch? *How many witches live in this land?* Oz was beyond confused. Clearly, someone was not telling him something.

Sensing his confusion, Glinda took him by the arm and began to explain everything. "Evanora is the true Wicked Witch. As conniving and cruel as they come. She's fooled 'most everyone, including her own sister. She made everyone believe I poisoned my own father, but it was she."

"Then . . . she's the one who destroyed my village?" China Girl asked.

Kneeling down, Glinda told China Girl the truth—it had been Evanora who had sent the baboons to destroy her village. The baboons were her minions, bent on destruction. But China Girl didn't want to be comforted, and pulled her hand away as Glinda tried to hold it. There was an awkward silence until Finley decided to break the ice.

"Here's your wand," he said, handing her back her magic wand. "Sorry I mooed," he confessed. Then he turned toward Oz. "And to think you almost killed Glinda for a bit of gold," he said.

"A bit? There were *mountains* of—!" He caught himself. "Not that I was going to do it. I wasn't really going to break your wand."

"Follow me," Glinda said in a soft but commanding way. As she made her way through the cemetery gates, Oz, Finley, and China Girl followed, unsure of what was to happen next.

BACK INSIDE THE EMERALD CITY PALACE, Evanora stood in the throne room, staring into a large crystal ball. She watched as Oz and Glinda met, and watched as the group entered the cemetery together.

"No, no, no! No, it cannot be!" Evanora screamed, even as her magic crystal ball proved that Oz had not defeated Glinda as Evanora intended. "Curse you, Glinda! Curse you and your pretty little face!"

Just then, Theodora ran into the room. "Sister!" she began. "Sister, the Wizard is missing!" Theodora was panicking. "I've looked everywhere, but he's gone. Where is the Wizard?"

"Where is the Wizard?" Evanora repeated as a new plan began to form in her evil mind. "With Glinda," she hissed, her voice cold. She gestured toward the crystal ball.

Moving closer, Theodora gazed into the ball's misty depths. She saw Oz and Glinda walking through the graveyard. Her eyes lit up. "Then it's happening!" she cried happily. "He's fulfilling the prophecy. He'll bring her darkness to the light and peace to the land."

Evanora bit her tongue. She wanted to shake her foolish sister, but that would not help. She had to think carefully about her next move. So much depended on what happened now.

After a few moments, she finally spoke. "Yes, I'm certain that's all it is," she said, her tone leading. "It must be. I just pray she hasn't fallen for his charms, too." Leaning down, she picked up a small jewelry box from under a nearby table. While hidden from view, Evanora whispered a few words and it magically transformed into one of Oz's music boxes. Standing up, she held it to her chest fondly.

Theodora's eyes flashed with confusion when she saw the box. "Where did you get that?" she asked.

"This?" Evanora replied innocently. "It was a gift, from him. He came to my chambers last night and oh, how we danced. For hours it seemed. You were right.

CHAPTER NINE

He is the great Wizard. He must be, to make me feel the way I did. . . ."

Her voice trailed off. Peering out from under her lashes, she waited to see if her words would work their own magic. Sure enough, Theodora's eyes had filled with tears. Her plan was working!

She kept going. "Oh, no!" Evanora said, feigning distress. "Not you, too, sister."

Theodora nodded sadly. "He said we would rule Oz together. He said I would be his queen."

"Did he?" Evanora asked, once again acting like the kind and caring big sister. She walked over and gently stroked Theodora's hair. Then she added, "Are you quite sure it wasn't *you* who said that to *him*?"

Theodora stopped sniffling as she recalled her conversations with Oz. Then her eyes grew wide. Her sister was right. He had never said those things. It had been her all along. She had thrown herself at him like a fool. Shame washed over her and she shrugged off her sister's touch, racing from the room.

Behind her, Evanora smiled with satisfaction. Her sister was angry at herself, true, but Evanora would use that anger. It might allow her to defeat Glinda once and for all.

But first, she would try another tactic. Throwing open the balcony doors, Evanora emerged into the night, her eyes wild. Calling to her winged baboons, she gave her orders. "I want Glinda and that Wizard torn to shreds! Do not fail me a second time! Fly!"

As she watched, the sky grew gray with the bodies of hundreds of baboons. In a swarm, they took off, heading south.

Unaware of the danger flying their way, Glinda had led the group to a large statue on one of the graveyard's hills. It was a statue of a king, and underneath were engraved the words: HERE LIES KING PASTORIA—THE KIND AND STRONG.

"On the day my father died, we lost a kind and noble king," Glinda said, her voice soft and her eyes sad, "and a dark shadow was cast across this land. I've had to stand alone and watch as towns were destroyed, children were orphaned, and my heart was broken. I've been unable to protect the good people of Oz by myself." Gently, Glinda reached out and placed a hand on the grave.

Oz looked at her, at a loss for words. He had never been good at these kind of situations. China Girl, however, understood Glinda's loss all too well. Gently, she took the Good Witch's hand in hers.

Smiling down at her, Glinda continued. "With only faith in my father's prophecy, I've waited." She raised her eyes, looking directly at Oz. "For you, great Wizard from Kansas, to come and make things right."

The others turned to stare at him as well, and he felt the weight of responsibility sink on to his shoulders. "Yeah, about that . . ." he began. "You know, when I agreed to be king, I didn't realize how complicated all this—"

"She knows," Glinda said, cutting him off.

"What?"

"Evanora knows you know the truth now. Look."

Oz turned around and immediately wished he hadn't. There, on the horizon, was a horde of winged baboons. They were flying fast—right at them. And on the ground, a savage platoon of Winkie Guards charged forward. "What do we do?!" Oz cried.

"Wizard, now's the time," Glinda retorted. "Use your magic!"

Was she joking? There was no time for him to even try to pretend to do something magical. "Yes, uh . . . I think we should run!" Oz yelled.

Now it was her turn to be disbelieving. Was *he*

kidding? But when Glinda looked into his eyes, she saw pure terror. He wasn't kidding. And all her fears were confirmed. Turning to the others she screamed, "You heard the Wizard! Run!"

Finley and China Girl didn't hesitate. They took off through the graveyard. Behind them, the flying baboons and the Winkies closed in. Glinda waved her wand. A moment later, a thick fog began to sweep across the land enveloping everyone—including the baboons.

"Is that going to stop them?" Oz yelled.

"I don't know!" Glinda yelled back.

Suddenly, everything went silent, and there were no flying baboons or Winkies in sight. "Nice work," Oz said. "We lost them."

"That was close," echoed Finley. Then Glinda turned, nervous about some unforeseen force.

"Wait, I hear something," the Good Witch said. Suddenly, a winged baboon emerged through the fog with an earsplitting SCREEECH. The Wicked Witch's minions had found them.

Inside the thick mist, Oz turned frantically one way and then the other. He couldn't see a thing! He heard China Girl calling to him through the fog, her voice thick and muted. Making his way toward her, he picked her up and continued to run as baboons screeched all around him. Suddenly, he ran straight into one of the winged creatures. He let out a scream. So did the monkey. Stopping, Oz realized that he had run into Finley. This was Glinda's plan? To have them trapped in a blinding fog?

Finally, the four companions made their way up a steep hill and rose out of the fog. They found themselves standing on the edge of a cliff.

"What do we do?" Oz wondered.

"What do we do?" Glinda repeated. "Just do what I do," she said with a smile. She looked remarkably calm despite the circumstances. "Unless you've got something?" she wondered. But Oz just shook his head. Turning, Glinda stepped closer to the edge. Then, as Oz watched in horror, she jumped, disappearing into the fog.

"Wait! What are you doing?" Oz said, panicked. Then he saw Finley lift China Girl and approach the edge. "Where are *you* going?" he exclaimed.

"She said to do what she did," Finley calmly replied.

"Just 'cause she jumps off a cliff, you jump off a cliff?!" Oz yelled.

"I have wings," Finley said matter-of-factly.

"What about me?!?" Oz screamed.

"You'll be all right," Finley said. "You're a wizard."
And with that, Finley lifted China Girl off her porcelain
feet and jumped off the edge of the cliff.

"That's not funny!" Oz called out after him.

Oz was now all alone. Behind him, he could hear
the baboons growing closer. Panicked, he looked one
way and then the other. There was no choice. He
stepped out into the nothingness, let out a bloodcurdling
scream, and was swallowed up by the fog. A moment
later the baboons went soaring past overhead.

As soon as the baboons had disappeared, a huge
soaplike bubble rose out of the fog. Glinda was inside.
Two more bubbles followed, carrying China Girl and
Oz. Finley flew alongside.

"Look at me! I'm a bird! I'm flying!" said China
Girl, amazed at floating high above the land in a
translucent bubble.

Inside his bubble, Oz tried to get his bearings.
But every time he moved, the bubble would spin. He
had no control! As China Girl and Finley laughed, Oz
finally righted himself.

They floated up and above the thick mist until they

burst into the sunlight. Oz smiled as he looked around. It was sort of like flying in a hot-air balloon. Although he wasn't quite sure who was steering. Behind him, and to his left and right, was nothing but blue sky. But right in front of him, right where they were heading, he saw what looked like a sparkling, translucent wall. It stretched east to west as far as the eye could see. Everything on the other side appeared hazy, almost like a mirage.

"Is that a wall?" Oz asked.

"Of sorts," Glinda answered. "It repels our enemies and protects us from harm."

"But we're headed straight toward it!" Oz cried, his voice rising. "And going very fast. Does this thing have brakes? Oh, no! I'm going to die!"

Watching him bounce around and scream inside his bubble, Glinda tried not to smile. "You needn't worry, Wizard," she said. "It's a *magic* wall! All good-hearted souls get to pass through."

Oz stopped screaming. Right. A magic wall. That let *good* souls through. Wait a minute—he wasn't a good soul! He really *was* going to die! He began screaming again, waiting to be zapped with electricity or dropped out of the bubble.

Closer and closer they came to the wall. Oz closed his eyes and braced himself. He waited and waited. Nothing happened. Finally, opening one eye, he looked around. He was on the other side! Behind him, the others passed safely through the wall, causing it to shimmer and sparkle. Oz let out a sigh of relief.

In her own bubble, Glinda let out her own sigh of relief. She had been right. Oz *was* good-hearted. Now she just needed to figure out how to make him see that, before it was too late.

AS THEY FLOATED high above Quadling Country, Oz took in his surroundings. It was a beautiful land, full of rolling hills and picturesque farms. To his right, Oz saw water pouring out of a large moss-covered rock, and to his left huge trees with large, leafy canopies that soared high into the sky. Sneaking a peek at Glinda, Oz smiled slightly. It figured that someone as beautiful as Glinda would live somewhere as beautiful as Quadling Country.

Turning his gaze forward he saw that they were approaching a castle. It was perched on a hill, its sides gleaming white. Several large towers rose into the air, their roofs a soft blue color that matched the sky.

The bubbles began to sink closer to the ground. As

they did so, Oz noticed that hundreds of people had gathered on the road to the castle. And they were all cheering. "They've waited a long time for you," Glinda said to Oz.

Oz returned his gaze to the people below. They all looked so happy and excited. They were cheering and shouting, racing to the city to greet him. Or, rather, who they *thought* he was. Oz plastered a smile on his face. This was all an act, and he could be a very convincing actor.

At last, the bubbles made their way into the castle's courtyard. Gently, they dropped to the ground and then dissolved. The cheers grew even louder. "All hail Oz!" the crowd exclaimed.

"What, no fireworks?" Oz asked Glinda as she led them through the crowd.

"What are fireworks?" Glinda asked, confused.

Oz shook his head. "Remind me to show you sometime."

They pressed on, the swarming crowd making it difficult to walk. As they drew closer to the steps leading up to the palace, Oz cleared his throat. This was all too much. He needed to come clean. He had to tell Glinda the truth. There was no way he could save her people from the likes of Evanora. Wouldn't it be better to tell them now so they could run?

"Look," he said, whispering to Glinda. "There's something I should . . . well . . . I may not exactly be . . ." He paused. "A wizard," he finished.

He waited for Glinda to scream or hit him or faint in shock. But she just smiled. "Yes, I know. At least, not any kind of wizard we were expecting." She turned and waved at the crowd.

"You could tell?" Oz said, confused.

"Yes," Glinda replied. "I can also tell you're weak, selfish, slightly egotistical, and a fibber," she said.

"I see," Oz said, his ego bruised. "Anything you *don't* know about me?"

"Whether you'll save my people," she replied.

Oz paused. He had just told her he wasn't a wizard. He had no powers. And as she had clearly pointed out, he apparently had very few redeeming qualities. Turning to look at the crowd, he sighed. How was *he* going to save *them*?

Glinda began to make her way up the steps of the palace. "If you *make* them believe, then you are wizard enough," she said, her voice quiet. "These are desperate times, after all. Can you make them believe?"

Reaching the top, she turned and looked out over the crowd. Oz turned as well. It seemed all of Quadling Country was there, and they were all looking up at him with eager and hopeful eyes.

"Will I still get the gold?" Oz whispered out of the corner of his mouth.

Glinda sighed and rolled her eyes. But she gave a small nod.

Oz smiled. He had told the truth. His conscience was clear. Now it was time for the show to go on. He raised his arms. "Good people of Oz!" he cried. "Your Wizard is here!"

And the crowd went wild.

Through the crystal ball, Theodora watched Oz and Glinda greet the Quadlings. She fought back tears as they waved to the crowd and exchanged smiles. They looked so happy. Just like she and Oz had been once upon a time. . . .

As another tear rolled down her cheek, Evanora entered the throne room. Seeing her sister's weepy expression, Evanora rolled her eyes. "What's the matter, sister?" she said with a sigh.

"Look at how happy they are," Theodora said as she gazed into the magic crystal ball. "Do you think she'll be his queen?" she asked sadly.

Evanora sighed. Her sister was so softhearted. It was such a waste of a witch. If only she would stop hemming and hawing over Oz and focus on helping her destroy Glinda. But no, she just stood there, staring at the ball, wishing she were living some silly happily-ever-after.

"Of course she'll be his queen," Evanora finally answered, causing Theodora to gasp. It was cruel, but if Evanora's plan was to work, there could be no room for feelings. "Well, what did you expect?" Evanora said, leading her sister on. "You can't compete with Glinda's charms. No one can."

More tears welled in Theodora's eyes and she cried out in anguish. "Oh sister! It hurts!"

"It won't cease hurting, so get used to it!" Evanora replied harshly. "Such is a broken heart. Your precious *Wizard* did that to you!!"

Evanora's words bit into Theodora, breaking her heart anew. Was her sister right? Was this all Oz's fault? Had he worked some sort of magic on her, causing her heart to swell and then explode so painfully?

"Make it stop!" Theodora pleaded to her sister.

Seeing the doubts flit across Theodora's face, Evanora stifled a smile. This was just what she wanted. "I can help you, sister," she said, her voice growing more gentle. "But you must help me in return."

Theodora looked up, her eyes red and swollen. "How?" she asked.

Sensing that her sister was on the verge of breaking, Evanora reached out her hand gently. "Come, sister," Evanora said as she led Theodora into a separate room. Slowly, Theodora placed her hand in Evanora's. Her fate was sealed.

Evanora had been waiting for this moment a long time. Soon, the Land of Oz would be hers once and for all. Settling Theodora at a table in her sitting room, Evanora went to work. She produced a vial of potion and carefully began to drip its contents onto a shiny green apple, drop by drop.

Slowly, Evanora put the vial down and held up the apple. It was ready. "One bite is all it takes. One bite, and your world will change forever. One bite, and your heart will become impenetrable. One bite, and you and

I will finally share the throne. Unless you'd rather see Oz and Glinda there. . . ."

The last of Theodora's doubts vanished. Grabbing the apple out of her sister's hand, she took a savage bite.

Immediately, the potion began to work. Searing pain ripped through her body. She felt a fire begin in her belly, and then her body convulsed as the potion rushed through her veins, straight toward her heart. She pushed back from the table, clutching at her chest as she let out a shriek. Then a wave of realization crossed her face and she looked to her sister, scared and confused.

"You're the wicked one! Not Glinda!" Theodora said, still gripped by the pain. "Sister, you lied to me!"

"It's nice, isn't it? How clear everything becomes?" Evanora said, still calm as ever.

"What's happening to me?" Theodora cried as another wave of pain washed over her body.

"Oh, it's just your heart . . . withering away," Evanora said soothingly. "Fear not, Theodora, for soon you'll feel nothing at all. Except beautiful wickedness. . . ."

Theodora gasped, fighting for air as her body and face continued to contort. The pain was unbearable. It had to stop! She couldn't take much more. Suddenly, she sank to the floor, folding in over herself. As Evanora watched, her sister's breathing slowed and then, slowly, she lifted her head.

Gone was the beautiful young woman with ruby lips and porcelain skin. Her button nose was now hooked and her dimpled chin was now long and pointy. And her beautiful skin was gone. She was now completely green.

Reaching up, Theodora felt her chin and nose. She stood up and made her way to a mirror hanging on the wall.

Evanora recoiled, disgusted by her sister's new appearance. "Oh, sister. You're *hideous*. Fear not, I can cast an enchantment, and you'll look just the way you were."

Staring at herself in the mirror, Theodora shook her head. "No," she said. "This is who I am now. And I want him to see me like this, I want him to know that *he* was the one who made me this way."

She stopped and touched her nose one more time, taking in her new, grotesque appearance. Then, she let out an unsettling cackle. Yes! Oz would see *exactly* what he had done. The old Theodora was gone. She was now the Wicked Witch of the West!

INSIDE GLINDA'S LIBRARY, the Good Witch paced back and forth. Time was of the essence. She needed to get Oz up to speed and prepared—fast. As she moved across the room, he lounged in a chair, an amused expression on his face.

"It's imperative that you behave like the great leader they think you are," Glinda said. "Morale is essential if we have any hope of defeating Evanora."

"I assume you have a plan," Oz said.

Glinda shook her head. "*You* have a plan," she corrected. "You're going to lead us into battle, and take back the throne."

"I see," Oz replied. "And do we have an army to do this?"

There was a pause, and then Glinda answered, "Of sorts."

Oz narrowed his eyes. That didn't sound promising.

And he was right. It wasn't promising. Leading Oz outside, Glinda brought forth the assembled troops, if they could be called that, for his inspection. It was a ragtag group. First there were the Quadlings, who were farmers, not fighters. As they offered to bake bread, hoe land, and even make scarecrows, Oz felt his hope for an easy victory begin to fade.

Next up were the Tinkers. Unlike the Quadlings, who were short and stout, the Tinkers were tall, thin, and for the most part, decrepit old men. They had long white beards and pointy ears. Seeing the doubt in his eyes, Glinda spoke up. "What they lack in stamina, they make up for in ingenuity. The Tinkers can build *anything.*" Oz held back another groan. How could they build things when half of them couldn't hear and the other half looked like they could barely stand?

Glinda led Oz to the last group. "And finally, the Munchkins," she said, gesturing to rows of little people dressed in very frilly clothes.

"Ah. You saved the best for last," Oz said sarcastically.

The Munchkins all began to giggle.

"What did I say?" Oz asked, confused.

"Nothing," Glinda replied. "They do that when they're nervous."

Perfect. That would be extremely helpful on the battlefield. "Do *any* of you fight?" he asked.

One of the Munchkin women stepped forward. "No," she said. "But we can make pretty clothes."

Then a Munchkin man spoke up. "Also, we sing."

Without warning, the Munchkins broke into song and began to dance around the courtyard. "The prophecy was clear! The wind would bring you here! And so it was, a man named Oz, did magically appear!"

Oz watched, unsure of what to do. When the Munchkins started a second verse, Oz yelled to them to stop. The Munchkins instantly grew quiet . . . and then they all began to giggle again.

This was ridiculous. There was absolutely no way he was going to be able to lead any of these people into battle. "Wanda—" he began.

"Glinda," she corrected.

He nodded. "*Glinda*, these are all lovely people, but do you honestly think they can kill a witch and an army of flying baboons?"

Glinda shook her head. "I don't expect them to kill anyone."

"What do you mean?" Oz asked.

"I mean, the good people of Oz are forbidden to kill, even in battle," she answered.

Oz shook his head. Had he just heard what he thought he heard? Pulling Glinda aside, he leaned in close. "You want me to lead an army," he whispered, "that can't kill?"

She nodded. "If it was easy, we wouldn't need a wizard, would we?" she said.

So the Witch's army could kill but his army could not? He hadn't expected this to be a walk in the park, but he didn't think the odds would be so much in the enemy's favor. And while Glinda had power, he was only a fake wizard. . . .

Suddenly, a Quadling woman screamed out and pointed up into the sky.

"Look! The Wall!" exclaimed a Munchkin man.

Oz and Glinda looked at the horizon. Sure enough, the translucent wall that protected Quadling Country was buckling as a glowing ball of fire pushed against it, causing the wall to sparkle and crackle.

"The Wicked Witch isn't powerful enough to get through the Wall!" Glinda said, confused at what was happening.

"Looks like she's managing," Oz replied as the fireball intensified.

Glinda was silent for a moment, her face serious. "She's not," she finally said. "Not by herself she isn't."

"What does that mean?" Oz cried. "Is someone *helping* her?"

Glinda didn't have time to figure that out now; she had to act fast to protect her people. "Everyone, take cover!" she yelled. "Hurry! Get the children to safety!"

Just then, Oz looked up to see the huge fireball burst through the wall—and it was hurtling straight toward them. Oz quickly pushed Glinda out of the way as the fireball smashed into the town square with a thunderous explosion. Smoke filled the center of the square, sending Munchkins, Tinkers, and Quadlings racing for cover.

When the smoke and fire cleared, Theodora stood in the rubble of yellow bricks that had been the town square. Her bright red coat was gone, replaced by a black dress and a tall, pointy black hat. She looked around at the crowd, which stared back at her fearfully. The Wicked Witch of the West had arrived.

"There's so much good here," Theodora said as she looked around. "It sickens me!" she hissed as the crowd recoiled in fear. "Still think your Wizard can save you? From the likes of *me*?" she asked. She sniffed the air with her long green nose then turned and lunged at a terrified Quadling. "Speak up, or I will tear out your tongue!" she ordered.

Oz was baffled. He thought he had met the Wicked Witch already. Was Glinda not telling him everything? "Now who is *that*?" he asked, leaning over and whispering into Glinda's ear.

But his whisper wasn't much of a whisper and Theodora heard every word. "Don't you recognize me, Wizard?" the green woman asked. "Have I really changed so much?"

"Theodora?" Oz asked in disbelief. This woman could not be the lovely and innocent woman he had met in the forest. This woman was cruel and heartless . . . and very, very green.

"May I have this dance?" the Wicked Witch asked.

Then, with a wave of her hand, Oz was lifted off the ground. He spun in the air several times—over and over and around and around—as though twirling to unheard music.

"Theodora, stop!" yelled Glinda. "You're hurting him!"

The Wicked Witch of the West glared at Glinda. Then, with another wave of her hand, the Witch sent Oz flying across the square. He landed with a thud on the cobblestones. Shaken and bruised, he looked up, his eyes filled with confusion and pain.

"Theodora?" Oz asked. "What . . . happened to you?" he stammered.

"YOU happened to me!" she roared, raising her hands as if to strike at him again.

But before she could, Glinda waved her hand, blasting Theodora with a powerful gust of wind. "This isn't you, it's your sister," she said. "She worked her evil on you. I'd hoped you'd see through her."

Theodora sneered at Glinda. "I never liked you, Glinda. It's such a relief that I don't have to pretend anymore!"

That was all that the Quadlings had to hear. The Witch might have tormented the Wizard, but the good people of Oz were not about to let this Witch speak against their Glinda. Grabbing a broom, a Quadling woman brandished it menacingly before the Wicked Witch. And soon, she was soon joined by other Quadling women, all of whom stood against Theodora. "Begone, Witch!" the woman with the broom yelled. "Before the Wizard makes mush of you!"

"You all believe in him," the Witch began. "Well, so did I . . . once."

"No, you just got the wrong idea—" Oz tried to explain.

"I opened my heart!" the Witch quickly retorted. "And you crushed it!" she said with an angry scream. Taking a moment to compose herself, Theodora continued. "That will never happen again," she said to him before turning her attention back to Glinda and her people. "As for you, my pretty one, when I return with my sister and her army, the Yellow Brick Road will be red with the blood of every farmer, Tinker, and Munchkin in your kingdom," she threatened.

"You underestimate us," Glinda replied. "We are a strong and united people. Now the Wizard will lead us."

But Theodora knew the truth about Oscar. "As for your Wizard," she said to the crowd, "if he has not run away by tomorrow, he will be the first to die.

And you will all see that he is nothing but a deceitful, selfish, and extremely mortal man."

Theodora turned to the Quadling woman with the broom and grabbed it from her hands. "It was a broom you wanted, wasn't it, Wizard?" she hissed. And with a loud cackle, she jumped on the broom and flew away, leaving a stunned crowd behind.

Glinda immediately tried to console the frightened crowd. "It's all right, she's gone now," she said. "Don't be afraid. Now that the Wizard is with us—" But her voice just trailed off. The Wizard named Oz was gone.

As soon as Theodora—who was now known as the Wicked Witch of the West—flew away, Oz took off, too. Enough was enough. He had thought he was in over his head, but now he was certain. He had two Wicked Witches very angry at him, and one Good Witch with an army of people who couldn't fight who expected *him* to fight their battle for them. He knew when the show was over—and this show was definitely over!

Racing into his room, he grabbed his satchel. He clutched it to his chest as he ran down a long hallway.

But just when he was about to reach the large double doors that led to freedom, they began to open magically by themselves. Glinda was standing on the other side, hands on her hips.

"Where do you think you're going?" she asked.

Oz let out a sigh. "Look, obviously there's been a terrible misunderstanding."

"You promised to help us," Glinda said, cutting his protests off.

"I know, but I'm only making things worse!" he shouted, losing his temper. "Before you had one Wicked Witch, and now you have *two*."

"That's all the more reason to stay and fight," Glinda said, unswayed.

The woman was infuriating! Was she so stubborn that she couldn't see how bad off they were? They had an army of fossils and bumpkins. "I'd like to stay and help," he finally said. "But I can't." He pushed past her, heading for the exit. "Good luck, Glinda."

Glinda waited a moment. "Very well," she said, just as he was at the door. "I'll be sure to send word to the sisters that you're no longer under my protection."

Oz stopped in his tracks. He turned and looked her in the eye. Nope, she wasn't bluffing. "Now why would you do that? You might as well sign my death sentence."

"The choice is yours, Wizard," she answered.

He was defeated. There was no choice now. He would have to stay and fight if he at least hoped to live. If he didn't, it was certain death. He narrowed his eyes. "And you call yourself a *good* witch . . ."

EVANORA STOOD ON HER BALCONY and looked out at hundreds of her Winkie Guards. They were sharpening their pikes on grinding wheels, throwing sparks up into the night. Meanwhile another battalion was marching into the courtyard, their spikes at the ready. The Wicked Witch was pleased. Her army would be ready to fight and defeat Glinda and her people. As Theodora joined her, Evanora called down to her guards.

"My very own Winkie Guards! Soon you will be facing Glinda and her army of weaklings. When they see our towering might, they will run and flee!"

"No!" Theodora yelled, interrupting her sister. "We shall not let them flee! We shall show them no mercy!" With that, the Winkie Guards let out a massive and deafening roar. And as Theodora gave them an evil smile, Evanora looked over at her sister and wondered just what kind of monster she had created.

Oz had been given no choice but to *make* a decision. And now he was going to lead a ragtag army into a war against two powerful and wicked witches—one of whom had a very personal reason for seeing him fail. Which meant he needed a battle plan.

Night had long since fallen on Quadling Country as Glinda and Oz stood in her library preparing. In actuality, Glinda was preparing. Oz was just listening, growing more bored and more tired by the minute.

"These four roads all lead into the Emerald City," she explained, pointing to a map of Oz spread out on a table. A blazing fire burned in the fireplace behind the table, sending shadows dancing across her face as she went on. "They'll expect us to be coming from the south. To the east are the Deadly Poppy Fields—we'll have to steer clear of them."

"Why's that?" Oz asked.

"One good whiff, and it's everlasting sleep," Glinda replied.

Oz let out a big yawn. Sleep sounded really good

at the moment. He couldn't remember the last time he had had a long night's rest. Was it back in Kansas? He plunked down in an armchair and closed his eyes.

"Can't you at least *try* to participate?" Glinda asked.

"Not at this hour, no," he said, keeping his eyes closed.

Shaking her head, Glinda went back to studying the map. At least *one* of them should be prepared. But her thoughts kept drifting back to Oz. He was such an infuriating man. Still . . . She peeked over at him, slumped in his chair. His dark hair was tousled and his body was long and lean. There was something about him. . . .

"When they said 'wizard', they should have been more specific," she said under her breath.

But Oz heard her. "Just what kind of wizard were you expecting?"

That was easy. She was expecting the complete opposite of the man sitting before her. "Someone who is noble . . . inventive. Who puts others before himself. Brave, tall . . ." she said.

"I'm tall," Oz said, almost pouting.

An awkward silence filled the room. It was broken

by the sound of someone in the doorway. Turning, Glinda and Oz saw China Girl.

"Someone needs to tuck me in," she said, looking up at Oz with big, pleading eyes.

"Oh. Of course, allow me," Glinda said.

"But my papa used to do it," China Girl replied.

"I see," Glinda said, realizing. "Well, maybe you'd prefer the Wizard, then?"

He started to protest but the words died on his lips. China Girl looked so hopeful. And he knew Glinda was thinking he would never do it. But he would show her. Nodding, he reached out and took China Girl's hand.

Moments later, she was all tucked in. Thinking his job was done, Oz turned to go. But China Girl wasn't quite ready for sleep.

"Do you grant wishes?" she asked. He looked at her blankly. "The old Wizard could grant wishes. People would travel to the Emerald City to ask for things, and if they were good and noble wishes, the Wizard would grant them." She stopped speaking and her eyes grew sad. "You know what I'd wish for? To have my family back."

Looking down at the little girl, Oz's face softened.

"I know. I'm sorry. I can't grant wishes," he said. "I'm not that kind of wizard."

China Girl thought this over and then nodded. "That's what I thought."

Oz stood there awkwardly, unsure of what to do next. Then he sat down on the bed next to her and began to speak. "You see, where I come from, there aren't any real wizards," he said. "Although," he started again, "there is one. Thomas Alva Edison, the Wizard of Menlo Park. A truly great man."

"Did *he* grant wishes?" China Girl asked.

Oz shook his head. "No, but he could look into the future—and make it real," he said. "He invented the electric light, and the phonograph, and a camera that lets you take moving pictures."

The little girls eyes grew wide. "Pictures that move?" she asked, amazed.

Oz was getting into this story. "Can you imagine?" he said, nodding. "Made from old wires and glass bulbs. With almost nothing, he made the impossible happen!"

"Is *that* the kind of wizard you are?" China Girl said, letting out a loud yawn.

"It's the kind of wizard I'd *like* to be," Oz answered honestly.

Pulling up her blankets, China Girl snuggled down under the covers. "You *are* that kind," she said. "I can tell. I'd rather you granted wishes, but that's a good wizard, too." Rolling over, she closed her eyes.

For a moment, Oz just sat there lost in his own thoughts as he watched China Girl drift off to sleep. First Glinda with her opinions, and now a little girl made of china telling him he could be good. What a night.

A few minutes later, Oz stood in the doorway to Glinda's library. It had taken a girl made of china, but he was ready now finally to accept his role. He was willing to take this chance—for real. Now he just needed to tell Glinda.

Walking into the room, he found her sitting in a chair, her nose deep in a book. "Glinda! I've got it!" Oz exclaimed, but Glinda didn't know what he was talking about. "I've got a way out of this mess. Look, I know I'm not the Wizard you were expecting, but I might just be the Wizard you need." And for the first time in a long time, hope returned to Glinda's eyes.

OZ MARCHED INTO THE TINKERS' WORK-shop with a set of blueprints rolled up under his arm. He stood in the center of the room and called all of the Tinkers to gather around. Oz unrolled his blueprints and began to bark out orders. "This is what you're going to build. Where I come from it's called a praxinoscope, though I've made a few modifications. It allows you to project an image through space."

"Impossible!" the Master Tinker said.

"Nothing's impossible if you believe," Oz said.

"Bully!" the Tinkers cheered in unison. It was time for them to get to work!

After hours of work, Oz and the Tinkers had moved on to basic stagecraft, with the magician from Kansas teaching the Tinkers some trade secrets. "In the conjuring business, flash is always good. Gives the audience a little 'wow,'" he said.

Nearby, Finley put on some protective goggles, worried that there might just be too much flash.

As Oz continued to speak, he combined several different ingredients into a pot over the fire, which caused a bright and impressive flash before them that made them all jump.

Meanwhile, on the other side of the factory floor, Glinda the Good surveyed the scene and walked past rows and rows of Munchkins, all of whom were hard at work at sewing machines, making clothes and stuffing hay into burlap sacks.

Oz then directed a group of Munchkins who worked in an assembly line. One set of Munchkins loaded powder into tubes, while another set sealed the tubes, and yet another set attached the fuses. Oz gave them a satisfied smile. His fireworks were almost ready.

Oz was happy with the work. They were making progress—fast. Which was good, as they didn't have much time to waste. "Good work, gentlemen," Oz said. "Let's see that teamwork on the battlefield, all right?"

As Oz shook the hands of the workers, Glinda watched from afar, proud of the man Oz was becoming.

...............................✣...............................

After making sure the Munchkins were on schedule, Oz made his way back to the Tinker workshop. He had asked the Master Tinker to work on something special—his own version of Edison's projection screen—and wanted to see how it was coming along.

The Master Tinker was excited to show off his work. "Now I've added this adjustable lens to your design, as well as a few other things. Have a look," the workman said as he rotated the lens turret so that a new lens snapped down in front of the camera.

Oz nodded, looking over the machine. "Yes! Edison himself would be proud," he said, pleased with the results.

Putting his arm around the old man, Oz led the Tinker off, and whispered into his ear. "Do you know how to make a hot-air balloon?" Oz asked as they disappeared down a long hallway.

...............................✣...............................

Dawn rose over Quadling Country. The time had come. The Tinkers had finished tinkering, the Munchkins had finished sewing, and the Quadlings had used all the hay they could find. Inside the castle courtyard, everyone made last-minute preparations.

Oz and Glinda watched as the horses were hitched to their carts. "This is all very impressive, but you still haven't told me how we're getting all this into the Emerald City," Oz said.

"Relax," Glinda said. "I know someone."

What did she mean? Whom did she know? Oz wondered. As if on cue, Oz heard a voice from behind him. "Hello, Wizard," the voice said. Oz turned around to see Knuck the Munchkin. As usual, he was scowling up at him.

"Well, whaddaya know, if it isn't ol' Sourpuss!" Oz said with a smile.

"My name is Knuck!" the Munchkin said in his usual unhappy demeanor.

"You two be nice to each other," Glinda said, moving between them. Knuck and Oz exchanged a few more barbs, then the Munchkin walked off, leaving Oz standing alone with Glinda.

"Guess I'm up," Oz said to Glinda. "Gotta do what I do. Cue the con man."

Glinda frowned. "Would you stop?" Glinda said,

frustrated that Oz was being so hard on himself. "A con man couldn't have done all this."

Glinda moved in close and removed his hat. "You're much more than that," she said softly. For a moment, both Wizard and Witch were silent as they looked at each other. So much had been said and yet so much was left unsaid. Glinda knew that there was a good chance Oz would still try to run. Oz knew it, too. It felt like something was ending that had never had a chance to start.

Then, slowly, delicately, Glinda leaned over and kissed him on the forehead. "For protection," she said. "Not that you'll need it."

Oz stood on the Yellow Brick Road outside Glinda's castle. The sun shone brightly on the ragtag army of Quadlings, Munchkins, and Tinkers. With everyone together in one spot, Oz decided that he needed to give his troops a rallying speech.

"Great people of Oz," Oscar began, "today we fight to free the land from the villainy of the Wicked Witches. We are few, but we are mighty. Quadlings, Tinkers, Munchkins. We face great odds, but we are armed with our courage, our hard work, and most of all . . . our faith in one another," Oz said. "We have nothing to fear as long as we believe! For when we believe, anything is possible. Onward!"

The army released a mighty roar, and Oz smiled. For the first time ever, he actually looked and behaved like a great man. Even China Girl, Finley, and Glinda saw the change in him. They all watched with pride.

Oz divided the army into thirds, with each group heading down a different part of the Yellow Brick Road toward the Emerald City. Glinda smiled to herself. Maybe, just maybe, they would defeat the Wicked Witches after all.

A SHORT WHILE LATER, the wagon pulling the projection machine, which had since been covered by a tarp, pulled up to the Emerald City's back gate. The Gate-Keeper stepped in their path, blocking them. "Halt!" he yelled out and the wagon stopped.

Knuck sat in the driver's seat. Next to him was what appeared to be a Winkie. The man was tall, like a Winkie. And he had a typical Winkie hat and coat on. But he looked, well, lumpy. Which wasn't surprising. The Winkie was actually Oz in disguise. He was riding on a Munchkin's shoulders as part of his disguise. He held his breath as they came to a stop. He hoped that the Gate-Keeper had poor vision.

"Good day there, fellow Winkie Guardsman," Oz said in his deepest Winkie voice.

"What is your business here?" the Gate-Keeper inquired.

"We bring supplies for the battle," Oz said.

"I was told of no such delivery," the Gate-Keeper said, eyeing Oz suspiciously. That was one strange-looking Winkie. "Where are your papers of transit?"

Knuck didn't like where this was going. If the Gate-Keeper kept asking questions, or worse, asked them to get down, Oz's cover would be blown. It was time to move on, so Knuck used his walking stick to knock the Gate-Keeper in the head. "Why this delay?" he said, his voice angry. "Do you not recognize me? I am Knuck! The City Herald!"

"Sir, I'm just trying to do my—" the Gate-Keeper said before he was clunked on the head a second time with Knuck's walking stick. That was all it took. The Gate-Keeper began to scramble around, frantically trying to open the gates. "What I meant was, let them pass!" he said apologetically.

A moment later, the gate opened and Knuck waved the carts on. As they entered, Knuck couldn't resist clunking the Gate-Keeper one more time . . . so he did. Soon, all of them were inside the city as the gate closed behind them. Oz let out a sigh of relief. Part one was complete.

Inside the palace walls, the next phase of the plan was about to begin.

The Projection Wagon was wheeled into a back alley of the Emerald City, where it encountered a group of Munchkins. Oz thought they had been discovered until Knuck informed him that these men were the Emerald City Underground, and that they were on their side. "Everything is ready," Knuck told Oz as he leaped out of the wagon. "All we need now is you."

Shrugging out of his disguise, Oz nodded. "All right, I just have to do one thing first."

"There's no time," Knuck said. And that's when it hit him. That's when he knew.

Knuck glared at Oz as his expression changed and disappointment washed over his face. "I told Glinda you'd do this," he said. "She said I was wrong about you. Guess I wasn't."

"What are you talking about?" Oz asked.

"I'm talking about that thing the Tinker built. The balloon," Knuck replied.

"What balloon?" asked Finley, who had been riding in the back of the wagon.

122

Oz couldn't bring himself to answer Finley, or look either Finley or Knuck in the eye. Instead, he turned and looked toward the Room of Resplendence and saw the hot-air balloon moored to the bridge that led to the room. This was his chance, he thought. It was now or never.

"That's my cue," Oz said as he began to walk toward the balloon. Then he turned and looked back toward Finley and Knuck. "All right, you guys, just remember, stick to the plan."

"Stick to the plan!" Finley said, growing more and more agitated. "The plan was *you*! We're supposed to stick to *you*!"

"You guys will do great," Oz said. "So long." And with that, Oz ran off toward the hot-air balloon, ready to escape the land of Oz once and for all.

On the edge of the forest that bordered the poppy fields stood Glinda the Good. She looked out beyond the expansive poppy fields to the shining Emerald City. Then, raising her wand, Glinda formed a thick, low-hanging fog around her. With another wave, the fog grew, and slowly rolled downhill, covering the entire poppy fields.

On their perch, the Wicked Witches watched as a low, thick fog began to spread across the poppy fields. The fog troubled Theodora, but Evanora was not worried. A fog of that size required substantial effort from a witch. Even a witch as powerful as Glinda, who was most certainly behind it, could not keep it up forever. And the longer it lasted, the weaker Glinda would become.

The sisters continued to watch. At first, all they could see was the fog, but then, slowly, they heard the sounds of an approaching army. "They dare march upon us!" Evanora yelled.

Soon, they began to see the faint outline of figures making their way over the hill. Row upon row of soldiers marched in formation, heading toward the Emerald City.

Theodora raised her arms and the skies turned black as hundreds of flying baboons swooped overhead. They were headed directly for the battlefield below.

Watching her army attack, Theodora smiled. "Tear them apart!" Theodora yelled. She let out a terrifying cackle that gave Evanora the chills. Something was definitely wrong, the older sister thought. Then she turned her attention back to the battle.

CHAPTER FOURTEEN

Evanora looked concerned. She watched as the baboons descended into the poppy fields and began ripping the army to pieces, tearing anything they could get their hands on. It was a massacre . . .

Except, there was no blood.

Horror washed over the sisters' faces as they realized the truth. "It's a trick!" Evanora shouted. "Retreat! Retreat!"

Her army didn't listen. The baboons continued their attack. But as the fog began to clear, the baboons looked down and realized they weren't attacking Munchkins or Quadlings . . . they were attacking scarecrows! Rows and rows of scarecrows were propped up on rolling racks, the hay inside them now spilling out. Turning, the sisters' army began to flee.

But it was too late. . . .

Glinda's plan had worked—while the winged baboons were tearing up the scarecrows, the Good Witch's fog had raised the poppy dust all around them. The baboons breathed it in, and soon fell over into a deep, deep sleep.

Glinda, China Girl, and the Quadlings cheered. It was now time to put the next part of their plan into action.

AS THE LAST OF THE FOG cleared from the poppy fields, the Wicked Witches spotted Glinda and the others at the forest's edge.

"Curse you!" yelled Theodora. But Evanora knew that the battle was far from over. She turned and saw Oz's balloon floating down to the Room of Resplendence. The magician was escaping, but he was going to get some gold first. Evanora's fingers crackled with electricity. The Witch wasn't about to let him steal her gold. As she reared back, ready to fire a blast of energy from her fingertips, Theodora steadied her hand.

"No, sister. The Wizard is mine," she said. "You take care of Glinda."

CHAPTER FIFTEEN

Meanwhile, at the edge of the Enchanted Forest, unaware of Oz's betrayal or that they had been discovered by the witches, Glinda was rallying the army and readying supplies. "Quadlings, fall back!" she instructed. "The fog is lifting. Into the woods!"

Suddenly and without warning, two huge winged silverback baboons swept down and lifted Glinda off her feet.

Before anyone could react, they had carried Glinda high into the air. She raised her wand to defend herself, but then Evanora appeared. Glinda didn't have a chance. The Wicked Witch zapped her with a bolt of electricity and as everyone watched in horror, Glinda lost her grip on the wand and it dropped toward the ground below. Powerless and defeated, Glinda was carried away. . . .

Evanora searched the grass for the missing wand, but it was nowhere to be found. Frustrated, Evanora rejoined the baboons as they returned to the Emerald City.

Meanwhile, hiding behind a tree was China Girl. She clutched Glinda's wand to her chest. She was scared, but she knew she had to act. Summoning all her courage, she took off through the tall grass toward the Emerald City. She had to get to the palace . . . fast.

Oz, meanwhile, was only concerned with his future. He dashed across the bridge leading to the Room of Resplendence, past the repaired hot-air balloon waiting for him, and into the room filled with treasure. Opening the doors, he began snagging anything he could find. He saw bags of coins and grabbed those, throwing a few extra gems and pieces of jewelry inside. He wanted to get as much treasure as his little balloon could hold. Dragging it all outside, he heaved it over the side into the basket. Oz was ready to go, escape out of the Land of Oz, and fly back home with more riches than he had ever imagined. But as he looked over the bridge to the crowd below, he felt a pang of remorse. These people had trusted him to help them. Their fate was in his hands. It was time for a new plan.

Night had fallen on the Emerald City, causing the green of the buildings to take on a darker appearance. From the city's main square the citizens watched as the two flying silverback baboons dropped Glinda the Good onto the dais. Immediately, two Winkie Guards grabbed her and chained her up for all to see.

CHAPTER FIFTEEN

Evanora slowly floated down in front of her, making sure everyone knew who was really in charge. "Citizens of Emerald City," she began. "Witness what happens when you defy me." She landed on the dais and looked out at the frightened masses. "Glinda did very well for herself today, I'll admit—but that's all over now." Then she turned to look directly at Glinda. "So, what's next, do you think?"

"Get your sister and fly out of here," Glinda said defiantly. "While you still can."

This infuriated Evanora. "I think I'm going to do something quite different, and I'm going to do it very slowly because . . . I just can't stand that pretty, pretty face," the Wicked Witch said. "I'm going to wipe out your light until all that's left is my darkness. I've been waiting a long time for this."

Evanora raised her hands and bolts of electricity shot out from her fingertips at Glinda. The Good Witch screamed out in pain as the electricity coursed over her body. The Wicked Witch merely smiled. Then she fired again. "Seems as though your Wizard has vanished," she said with glee. "So much for your king and his worthless prophecy."

Oz's balloon was once again moored to the bridge next to the Room of Resplendence—only now, the balloon's basket was filled with gold. Oz hurried out of the room with even more gold in his hands, unaware that he was being watched from above by Theodora. "How predictable," the Witch said with an evil smile.

Meanwhile, China Girl had finally made it into the palace. Sneaking from one alley to another, she had just made her way past a group of Winkie Guards when she heard a terrible cackle from above.

Knuck and Finley heard the same cackle and also looked to the sky. It was the Wicked Witch of the West. She flew over the crowds on her broomstick and landed on the dais next to Evanora. "Give up, Glinda," she said. "Why do you continue to resist?"

"Because I believe in the Wizard," Glinda answered weakly.

"So did I once," Theodora said. "Behold!" the Wicked Witch said as she gestured upward, where Oz's balloon was rising into the distant sky.

All hope drained from Glinda's face as she saw Oz's balloon floating away from the Emerald City. Her greatest fears had come true. Oz really wasn't the good man she thought he was.

CHAPTER FIFTEEN

Glinda's disappointment spread through the crowd: Finley, Knuck, the Master Tinker, and the rest of the Quadlings and Munchkins could not believe their eyes as Oz's balloon drifted farther and farther away from the Emerald City. "Where's he going?" someone cried out. "He's abandoning us!" another person shouted.

Theodora smiled mysteriously. Then, raising her hand, she formed a huge fireball above her open palm. Then, with all her strength, she hurled it into the sky—and directly at the balloon.

From her spot on the platform, Glinda screamed as the fireball slammed into its mark. A moment later there was a loud BOOOOOM and the balloon exploded in a blinding blaze of light.

"Not so great and powerful after all," Theodora said with an evil gleam in her eye.

DOWN ON THE STREETS, the citizens of Oz looked up at the sky, their faces ashen. The Wizard had been killed. Now there was nothing to stop the two Wicked Witches from ruling the land. Even Glinda was not powerful enough to stop them without the Wizard's help.

Standing amid the crowds, China Girl had watched as the balloon lifted up and then watched as it had exploded violently. She clutched the Good Witch's wand tightly, unsure of what to do next.

Meanwhile, Finley stood in another part of the crowd. After everything they had been through, it was impossible to believe the fight was over. Although he hated to admit it, he had grown fond of Oz. Losing him was a crushing blow.

Suddenly, he felt a hand on his shoulder. "Hello, Monkey," a familiar voice said.

Turning, Finley's eyes lit up as he saw Oz standing before him. "Oz! I thought you were dead," the flying monkey said with hushed excitement.

"You were crying pretty hard. Is that for me?" Oz said with his usual charm.

"Some smoke got in my eyes," Finley retorted. But it was time for them to get back to business. "You fooled everybody," the monkey said. "That was your greatest trick yet."

"That was just the opening act," Oz said. He glanced over his shoulder and Finley followed his gaze. He saw Knuck and the Master Tinker standing by the Projection Wagon. They were at the ready. "It's showtime," Oz said.

On their pedestal, Evanora and Theodora stood, addressing the crowds. They had dragged a weak and beaten Glinda out with them and had propped her up between the two of them. They needed the citizens to see there was no hope. No one could save them now.

"Let this be the final word then!" Evanora shouted. "Your prophecy is dead! Like the king that spoke it! And the Wizard who tried to fulfill it!"

Theodora then addressed the crowd. "And now they'll be joined in death by dear Glinda the Good!" She turned and looked at the Witch. "Farewell, my pretty one!"

"Say hello to your daddy for me," added Evanora.

A huge fireball formed in Theodora's hands while blue electricity sparked between Evanora's fingertips. The Wicked Witch sisters raised their hands and prepared to strike the final deathblow.

And then . . . the city went dark.

The three witches looked at each other, confused. This was not their doing. But then, who's doing was it?

Down in the main square, there was an explosion. Bursts of flame shot into the air and then smoke began to billow out over the citizens. There were confused murmurs from the crowd.

Before the smoke cleared, a booming voice filled the square. "FEAR ME NOT, GOOD PEOPLE OF OZ! FEAR ME NOT!"

Then, as everyone watched in disbelief, Oz

appeared in the smoke. His body seemed to float above the ground, almost transparent. The flames turned his skin a slightly red color and his features wavered in the smoke.

"IT IS I: THE GREAT OZ!" the Oz hologram said in his booming voice as more flames shot into the sky.

Up on the balcony, Glinda's face lit up, her hope returning. He wasn't dead! He hadn't left them! And he clearly had some sort of plan. If she weren't trapped on the balcony and he weren't just an image right now, she would kiss him!

Evanora and Theodora were not nearly as pleased. They were angry, and rather confused. "More tricks?!" Evanora cried down. "After everything? How dare you defy us?" she yelled.

"DARE?" the Oz hologram boomed back. "HOW DARE *YOU*, WICKED SISTERS! NO ONE DEFIES OZ!"

"Guards! Destroy him!" Evanora ordered. Obeying the Witch, the Winkie Guards charged at the hologram with their pikes. They threw long spears at the hologram, but they sailed harmlessly through, doing absolutely no damage. Oz let out a mighty roar that terrified the guards and sent them running in the opposite direction.

"Guards! Come back here this instant!" Evanora ordered, but it was too late. They were already gone.

"YOU THOUGHT YOU COULD KILL ME? ME!" Oz said before letting out a hearty laugh. "THANKS TO YOU, I HAVE SHED MY MORTAL SHELL AND TAKEN MY TRUE AND ETHEREAL FORM!"

Using the Wizard's appearance as a distraction, China Girl ran behind a cart, poised to return the wand to its rightful owner.

"I AM NOW MORE POWERFUL THAN EVER!" Oz continued. "I AM NOW INVINCIBLE!"

Theodora stared down at the image of the man who had caused her so much grief. Her eyes narrowed. She was sick of listening to him talk. No one was invincible, not even Oz. "I defy you!" she yelled. Then, conjuring up another fireball, she heaved it straight at the hologram. Instantly, Oz's image was engulfed in flames and he screamed and writhed in pain. On the ground, the citizens pulled back from the intense heat. And when the fire died out, the image of Oz was gone.

CHAPTER SIXTEEN

Up on their balcony, Theodora and Evanora let out triumphant cackles. "Beautifully done, sister," said Evanora.

Inside the Projection Wagon, Oz stood within a small circle. A curtain was pulled around it and he was surrounded by strange-looking cameras. The device allowed his image to be transposed out in the square. On the other side of the curtain, Finley stood in front of a switch that turned the contraption on and off. He anxiously waited for Oz to give him the signal. But Oz was playing up the suspense. This was all part of the act, and he knew just how to play to an audience.

"Oz, come on!" said Finley. "It's taking too much time!"

"Hold . . . hold . . ." he said, but the suspense was too much for anyone to bear. Finley, Knuck, and the Master Tinker looked at one another until they couldn't take it anymore.

"They think they're winning!" Finley exclaimed.

Then Oz gave him the signal. Finley pulled a lever as the Master Tinker flipped a few switches, but nothing happened.

"Turn it on!" said Oz.

"Ohh, we've got a loose wire," the Master Tinker

said. "And the screw's stuck!" This was not good. Thinking fast, Oz grabbed his all-purpose tool from his pocket and threw it toward the Master Tinker.

"Use this!" Oz exclaimed. The Master Tinker quickly tightened the screw and flipped some more switches.

Out in the square, there was another huge BOOM, and once more fire and smoke filled the air. When it cleared, just Oz's head hovered above the ground, huge and transparent. As everyone watched, it began to grow, getting bigger and bigger, and then it began to float into the air.

"No, it cannot be . . ." Theodora said in disbelief.

"YOU CANNOT DEFEAT ME! I AM IMMORTAL! I AM THE GREAT OZ!" Oz cried, his voice sounding like rolling thunder.

The good people of Oz erupted in cheers for their Wizard, but Oz's demonstration was far from over.

"WITNESS AND OBSERVE," the Wizard said. "AS I UNLEASH THE STARS!" Everyone raised their heads and looked up as a single streak of light zipped across the sky like a meteor. Then another. And another. Then more and more, until the sky was full of lights crissing and crossing, slashing the sky with their light.

CHAPTER SIXTEEN

All at once, it stopped.

Theodora and Evanora exchanged looks, each wondering if that was it.

Oz saw their expressions and smiled to himself. "BEHOLD!" he roared to the crowd.

And then, the heavens exploded!

The night filled with light as hundreds upon hundreds of fireworks exploded in a dazzling display. There were orange ones and blue ones, yellow ones that twirled and green ones that branched out across the horizon. The citizens of Oz looked up, both terrified and awed at the same time. The guards, thinking the fireworks were some sort of deadly weapon, took off, abandoning their posts. Meanwhile, the Munchkins who were setting off the fireworks outside the Emerald City continued their barrage. It was a display unlike any the Emerald City had ever seen.

Back on the dais, Glinda looked up and smiled. "So those are fireworks," she said to herself.

But Evanora watched the lights with a different reaction. "He *is* the Wizard," she said. Frightened, she abandoned her sister and ran back into the palace.

Inside the Projection Wagon, Knuck called out to Oz and the Master Tinker. "We got Evanora! She's on the run!" he exclaimed.

Upon seeing her sister retreat, Theodora screamed with rage. "Come back here, you coward!" she shouted.

China Girl used this time to make her move. She slipped past Theodora and ran up to Glinda, still clutching the Good Witch's wand.

"It's you!" Glinda exclaimed, surprised and overjoyed at seeing China Girl.

Enraged, Theodora formed two huge fireballs, one in each hand, and called out to the Wizard. "I may not be able to kill you," she shouted, "but I can kill the one you love!"

Theodora turned to face Glinda, but to her shock, Glinda was gone. Now more furious than ever before, Theodora hurled the fireballs directly at the hologram. As they soared through the image, the hologram laughed at her . . . and then fireworks shot out of its mouth directly at the Wicked Witch.

A 3-D explosion of red, white, and blue erupted around Theodora as Oz bellowed, "BEGONE, WICKED WITCH! BEGONE, FOREVERMORE!"

Frightened beyond belief, the Wicked Witch grabbed her broom and flew away from the dais. But while Knuck and the Master Tinker celebrated, Oz knew that this wasn't over yet.

"I know your wickedness is not your doing," the Wizard called after her. "And should you ever again find the goodness within you, you are welcome to return," he said, his voice full of sincerity and compassion.

"Never!" the Wicked Witch screamed. Then, with a bloodcurdling cackle, the Wicked Witch of the West disappeared into the night sky.

Evanora raced into the throne room and began grabbing her things. She needed to make a quick getaway. Turning, she let out a gasp. Glinda was there, sitting in the throne, waiting . . . her wand at the ready.

"Not so fast," the Good Witch said. "You and I aren't finished yet."

"You have the throne, Glinda!" Evanora replied. "What more could you want?"

"You can't give me that," Glinda said. "You took what mattered most to me—my father. I will never again feel the comfort of his kindness. But I'll settle for the freedom of his people."

Evanora nodded. "Of course, Glinda," she said, trying to appease the other witch. "At the very least, they deserve that."

But as she spoke, she was creating a charge of electricity. Whipping her hands out in front of her, blue light slammed into Glinda, throwing her back against the wall.

Glinda crawled to her feet, her body aching. Watching, Evanora smiled and began to circle the Good Witch. As she walked, her feet began to leave the floor, and soon she was floating around Glinda.

"What's the matter, Glinda?" Evanora asked, taking pleasure in Glinda's pain. "Out of bubbles?"

To Evanora's surprise, Glinda didn't panic or look scared. Instead, she stood up taller. "Don't need them," she said as she too began to float. "Bubble's just for show."

With a cry of rage, Evanora unleashed another bolt of electricity. Raising her wand, Glinda caught the bolt and then flung it straight back at Evanora. ZAP! Evanora slammed against the wall, causing her amulet to shatter.

"Nooooo!" Evanora screamed. "What have you done?"

Standing in front of Glinda was something that looked like Evanora, but much, much older. Without the power of her amulet, the Wicked Witch had rapidly aged and had been transformed into her true form—a ghastly, old, yellow-skinned hag.

Looking at the pitiful creature, Glinda nodded. "Now everyone will see you as you truly are," the Good Witch said. It was a fitting punishment. But there was still one thing left to do. "In the name of my father, I banish you from the Emerald City. Never to return."

Hanging her head, Evanora began to crawl off toward the balcony. But she wasn't going to go without one last fight. Spinning around, Evanora let out a shriek and charged at Glinda.

Startled, Glinda raised her wand. ZAP! A burst of energy shot out and hit Evanora square in the chest. The force was so strong that she was flung back out through the balcony doors and over the railing. Rushing over, Glinda watched as Evanora plummeted toward the ground. Just as she was about to smash into the ground, the last of her baboons swooped down and grabbed her in their hairy arms. Howling, they flew off into the night.

Glinda watched until they were nothing but specks on the horizon. Then, smiling, she turned and went back inside. She had to address her people. Then she had to go find a certain Wizard. At long last, they had won, and the good people of Oz were finally free.

SURROUNDED BY CHILDREN, Glinda sat on the steps and looked out at the Quadlings and Munchkins. "Good people of Oz!" she said, addressing the crowd. "I have here a missive from the Great Wizard himself! And I quote . . ." She lifted up a parchment and began to read. "'With little more than pluck and belief, we made the impossible happen. As your Wizard, I hereby decree that henceforth and hereafter the Land of Oz will forever be free!'"

The crowd let out a deafening roar. With one last wave, Glinda made her way inside, the cheers fading only slightly as she closed the balcony doors behind her. In front of her, the Master Tinker and Knuck were busy moving the projector into place in the middle of the room. China Girl and Finley looked on, intrigued.

"Okay," said the Tinker, "give it a try."

Knuck flipped a switch and suddenly, Oz's large, transparent head appeared. Smoke filled the room. Everyone laughed and began clapping. It worked! They had been nervous that moving things around would have made the machine inoperable, but the Tinker had worked his own form of magic. They would be able to use the machine over and over again.

Oz stepped out from behind a green screen in the corner of the room. Walking over, he joined the others. "Well, if it isn't the most beautiful witch in all of Oz. Hello, Glinda," he said with a smile.

"Hello, Wizard," she said with a smile of her own. Then she turned to address the Master Tinker. "Well done, Tinker! The machine is beautiful. It looks like it was made for this!"

"That's workmanship," he responded. "What you displayed is real courage. Your father would've been more than proud. He would have marveled at the woman you've become."

"Zim Zallah Bim!" Oz exclaimed, drawing everyone's attention. "Excellent work, everyone. And now we're ready!" he began. "Should anyone need to speak with the Wizard . . ." he said, nodding at the holo-gram. Everyone nodded. They understood. This was the only way that they could keep the citizens of Oz believing in their Wizard. It was a trick, true, but a trick for the better good, as Glinda had pointed out.

"Remember," Oz went on. "Our secret never leaves this room. Oscar Diggs died so that the Wizard of Oz could live. When those witches come back, and they *will* come back, believe me, we're going to need everyone to believe."

The group nodded solemnly. No one would ever say a word.

Oz smiled. "Good. And now, a few gifts."

"Gifts?" China Girl said, confused.

"You know I can't grant wishes," he replied, "so this'll have to do."

The group gathered around him, curious. Smiling, he turned and pulled out his satchel. He opened it.

"First, to the Tinker—the man who can make anything, I bestow upon you . . . my lucky, uh, thing-amajig." Reaching in, he pulled out his all-purpose tool. "May it assist you in the reconstruction of the Emerald City." He handed it to the Master Tinker, who held it up, examining it closely.

"I will treasure it forever," he said, touched. "Thank you for your faith in me."

Oz smiled. "And now for Sourpuss," he went on, turning to the Munchkin.

"My name is Knuck," the Munchkin said, his expression grim as always.

"And now for *Sourpuss*," Oz repeated, "I grant the thing you're in need of most."

Knuck cocked his head. What was he in need of most? Gold? Jewels?

"A smile," Oz went on, pulling out a smile made out of cardboard attached to a stick. He held it out to the Munchkin. "It is yours."

Knuck grumbled and tried to give it back, but Oz refused. He would make Knuck smile, one way or another.

Next, Oz turned to the flying monkey. "And for Finley," he said, all joking aside. "You stood by my side when any monkey in his right mind would've flown away. To you I give you something I've never given anyone." He held out his hand. "My friendship. Now you are my partner. You are my friend. For life."

Finley paused, touched. Then, he reached out and

took it, shaking hard. Oz grinned. "For life," Finley repeated, still shaking Oz's hand.

Next, Oz turned to China Girl.

She was looking up at him expectantly. His face softened. "I'm afraid I can't give you what I know you want most. All I have for you . . . is this . . ." He motioned to the others. "It's *us*. I know it's not the family you had in mind, but I can promise you, with all my heart . . ."

China Girl cut him off, leaping into his arms. She hugged him as hard as she could. "It's *perfect*," she whispered into his ear. "Thank you."

Tears pricked Oz's eyes and he blinked, trying to stop them. Then China Girl looked to Glinda. "I wonder what you're going to get," she asked.

"I don't need anything, child," she said.

"You better have something for Glinda," China Girl demanded of Oz.

"Why, of course!" he said. "I've saved the best for last! For you . . ." His voice changed, sounding once more like he was back at a carnival, hawking his show. "A sight envied by all! And viewed by none! You will be astounded by what you see . . ."

Taking her hand, he pulled her into the booth and

pulled the screen shut. It was barely big enough for one person, let alone two, so Oz and Glinda found themselves nose to nose.

"Oh my," Glinda said softly. "It's very tight in here."

Oz wiggled his eyebrows. "Isn't it nice?"

"I know what you're up to, Wizard," she said, smiling despite herself.

"What?" Oz asked, trying to sound innocent. "I'm giving you a tour. And I wanted to thank you."

Glinda looked up at him, her eyes big. "For what?" she asked softly.

"For opening my eyes," he said honestly.

"And what do you see?" she asked, smiling.

"That I have everything I ever wanted," he said in a whisper. And it was true. It had taken him traveling through a tornado and landing in another land to figure out what mattered most, but now he knew. Friends, family, a place to call home, and being a good man? That was all that mattered. There was no way he would ever turn his back on that . . . ever.

Silence filled the small room as they looked into each other's eyes.

"For the record," Glinda said, breaking the silence, "I knew you had it in you all along."

"Greatness?" Oz asked.

She shook her head, a grin on her face. "No. Even better than that. Goodness."

Oz grinned right back. He couldn't imagine being anywhere but right there, in that booth with a Good Witch named Glinda. It felt like he had known her his whole life.

Leaning forward, he brought his mouth closer to hers. He closed his eyes, waiting for that first kiss. And then . . .

"Hey!" China Girl said from outside the screen, "What are you doing in there?"

She heard hushed whispering and then Oz's voice came echoing out. "Nothing!" he called.

China Girl giggled and then skipped away. Inside the booth, Oz smiled. He could really get used to this whole screen thing. But first, he needed to get something out of the way once and for all. Something he had been wanting to do for a *very* long time. Turning back to Glinda, Oz leaned down and kissed her.

Bright and shiny
and sizzling
with fun stuff . . .

puffin.co.uk

WEB FUN

UNIQUE and exclusive digital content!
Podcasts, photos, Q&A, Day in the Life of, interviews
and much more, from Eoin Colfer, Cathy Cassidy,
Allan Ahlberg and Meg Rosoff to Lynley Dodd!

WEB NEWS

The **Puffin Blog** is packed with posts and photos from
Puffin HQ and special guest bloggers. You can also sign up
to our monthly newsletter **Puffin Beak Speak**

WEB CHAT

Discover something new EVERY month –
books, competitions and treats galore

WEBBED FEET

(Puffins have funny little feet and
brightly coloured beaks)

Point your mouse our way today!